Book Three

Kathleen Kelly
USA Today Bestselling Author

Highway
Royal Bastards MC Jacksonville, FL - Book Three

Kathleen Kelly
USA Today Bestselling Author

ISBN: 978-1922883148

Editing by Swish Design & Editing
Proofreading by Swish Design & Editing
Book design by Swish Design & Editing
Cover design by Crimson Syn
Cover Image Copyright 2024
First Edition 2024
Copyright © 2024 Kathleen Kelly
All Rights Reserved

DEDICATION

For all the readers of the Royal Bastards MC.
You don't know it, but I was ready to quit writing
until I released my first book in the Royal Bastards
universe, and your love for Creed and my words
motivated me to keep going.
Thank you <3

Enjoy x

Note For THE READER

Below is a list of the other club chapters listed in this book and their authors.

In order of appearance:

Ankeny, IA – **Kristine Allen**
St. Ives England – **Amy Davies**

Royal
BASTARDS
MC SERIES

SIXTH RUN

Kristine Dugger: *Crazy Psycho*
KL Ramsey: *Lost in Yonkers*
Barbara Nolan: *Loving Smoke*
Crimson Syn: *Tormented by Regret*
Elizabeth N. Harris: *Warden*
Liberty Parker: *Butcher's Destruction*
Morgan Jane Mitchell: *Hard Knox*
B.B. Blaque: *Royal Family*
Darlene Tallman: *Kraken's Release*
H.J. Marshall: *Roughstock*
Claire Shaw: *Tyres*
Kathleen Kelly: *Highway*
J. Lynn Lombard: *Jaded Red*
India R. Adams: *Praying for Fire*
Nikki Landis: *Grim's Justice*
Dani René: *REV*

Verlene Landon: *Snagged by Hook*
Kris Anne Dean: *Scorched Souls*
J.L. Leslie: *Worth it All*
Jena Doyle: *Blood and Whiskey*
K.D. Latronico: *Wherever I May Roam*
Sapphire Knight: *Toxic Biker*
Nicole James: *Taking What's Ours*
Rae B. Lake: *Sins and Paradise*
Kristine Allen: *Blade*
Roux Cantrell: *Hell Bent*
Daphne Loveling: *Deadly North*
M Merin: *Big Timber*
Amy Davies: *Seized by Solo*
J.A. Collard Author: *In Too Deep*
Elle Boon: *Royally Embraced*
Murphy Wallace: *Misery and Ecstasy*
Theta James: *Demon in the Shadows*
Chelle C. Craze & Eli Abbott: *Untitled*

Royal Bastards MC Facebook Group -
https://www.facebook.com/groups/royalbastardsmc/
Website- https://www.royalbastardsmc.com/

Royal
BASTARDS CODE

PROTECT: The club and your brothers come before anything else and must be protected at all costs.
CLUB is **FAMILY**.

RESPECT: Earn it and give it. Respect club law. Respect the patch. Respect your brothers. Disrespect a member and there will be hell to pay.

HONOR: Being patched in is an honor, not a right. Your colors are sacred, not to be left alone, and **NEVER** let them touch the ground.

OL' LADIES: Never disrespect a member's or brother's Ol' Lady. **PERIOD.**

CHURCH is **MANDATORY.**

LOYALTY: Takes precedence over all, including well-being.

HONESTY: Never **LIE, CHEAT,** or **STEAL** from another member or the club.

TERRITORY: You are to respect your brothers' property and follow their Chapter's club rules.

TRUST: Years to earn it... seconds to lose it.

NEVER RIDE OFF: Brothers do not abandon their family.

Chapter

GWEN

The roar of engines thunders through my bones as I step into the rally with my camera in hand. Leather-clad figures blur past, their bikes gleaming under the harsh sun. I raise my Nikon, eye to the viewfinder, capturing the raw pulse of the Royal Bastards MC.

Click. Two riders laugh, shoulders knocking. Brotherhood.

Click. A fist flies, connecting with a jaw. Conflict.

Click. An older member, face lined with stories, nods at a younger one. Mentorship.

"Nice shots?" The voice rumbles deep, close behind me.

I lower my camera and turn. Justice. He's a little too pretty and confident, and I can't help but think the nickname 'Peacock' would suit him better. The one I want, Highway, hasn't so much as tried to talk to me, so I entertain Justice. He's offered to take me to Okefenokee Swamp, and I've said yes.

"Could be," I reply with a smile.

He leans closer and looks at my camera. Holding it out but not letting go of it, I show him a few of my photographs.

"They look good." He touches my elbow. "Are we still good for the swamp?"

Nodding, I smile up at him. "Sure are."

"Cool. I'll pick you up at seven so we can get back for an early dinner?"

Moving out of his grasp, I say, "How about we see how the day goes?"

Nodding, Justice gives me another of his smiles and saunters away. He heads for Highway and says something to him. Highway frowns at him, and Justice laughs as he walks away.

Curious, I move to stand next to Highway, whose gaze is fixed on Justice's back. "You really don't like him, do you?"

Highway jumps and blurts out, "Justice is a peacock."

Laughing, I nod. "Because he struts around? You know that nickname suits him better than Justice. How'd he get Justice, anyway?" I put my camera to my face and snap a photograph of Highway.

"He has a pretty black-and-white way of looking at things with a level head in situations. Are you familiar with the term 'His own brand of justice?' Well, that's sort of how he got it."

"And you? How'd you get yours?"

He leans against his bike and pats the seat. "Hop on, and I'll show you."

Shaking my head, I glance at the men and women around me. "There's so much to capture here." I nod at Creed talking to Reaper. "Comradery." I put my camera to my face and snap a picture of a group of MC members huddled around a bike that's being repaired. "Intellectual conversations."

Highway barks out a laugh. "Intellectual?"

"Look how serious they all are."

"You have a different way of looking at things," states Highway.

"Not me, the camera." I cradle it in my hands. "It gives you a different perspective."

"Lucy says you work for *National Geographic*?"

"Sounds very impressive, doesn't it?" I laugh. "Sort of... I sell them photographs of things I find on my journeys."

"You travel a lot?"

"Yeah. Well, I used to." Holding up my camera a little higher, I say, "I'd better get back to it."

"Who are the photographs for?" he asks.

"For the Royal Bastards. Thought it might be nice to have some shots of all of you in the clubhouse or in your own environment."

"Ahh... the wild men in their natural habitat,"

Highway says with a bad English accent.

I laugh loudly. "Something like that."

"How's Lucy doing?"

"Good. She's healing nicely. Dad did an awesome job." My sister was hurt recently, but lucky for her, our dad is a plastic surgeon.

Highway gestures toward Reaper with a quick lift of his chin. "I'm surprised he's here and not with her."

"Oh, God, please don't say anything to him. He's driving Cel-Lucy crazy. She told him I need him here to protect me, or she wouldn't be able to rest." My sister's club name is Lucy. She was born Celeste and has made it very clear she's Lucy now, but sometimes I slip up.

"Is it hard to call her Lucy?"

"No. It suits her better but old habits."

The sound of a gunshot pierces the air. I jump and press myself against Highway. His arms immediately wrap around me.

"Jesus! Who did that?"

"They're blowing off steam, is all," he replies, chuckling.

Staring up at him, I ask, "So, not *at* someone, just having fun?"

"Yeah. Creed will put a stop to it. He won't want the cops showing up."

"We're in the middle of nowhere. Do you really think they'd come out?"

"Gunshot noise travels. Someone might report it. We don't need the heat." I put my hand on his chest and try to step out of his embrace. "Are you going on a date with Justice?"

Surprised, I lean back to stare into his eyes. "Sort of."

"Define 'sort of.' "

"He's taking me to the Okefenokee Swamp to get shots of the gators and some of the other wildlife."

"Ahh... wild animals in their natural habitat. For *National Geographic*?" Highway has a crease between his brows.

"For them or whoever else wants to pay me for them. Why do you ask?"

Highway pauses for a beat, then says, "I don't like you being alone with him."

Tilting my head to the side, I say, "Well, maybe you should have asked me first?"

"Yo, Highway!" Reaper is walking toward us. "Are you bothering my future sister-in-law?"

Highway's arms drop away, and he shakes his head. "Nah. The gunshot startled her, is all."

"Is that a fact?" Reaper asks with a smirk. "Really? I'm sure Lucy told me you told her you did a stint in Afghanistan. You'd think you'd be used to loud noises."

Blushing, I hold up my camera. "Better get back to it. And you, Reaper, should mind your own business." I smile at Highway and walk away.

5

There are women, men, and motorcycles everywhere. I pick my way through the crowd and take photographs of all of it.

Another gunshot sounds, then another. No one seems bothered, so I keep snapping away. The weight of my camera is a solid reminder of my purpose here, shifted against my chest as I lift it to my eye. Through the lens, life among the Royal Bastards MC sharpens into focus, a tableau of raw energy and unspoken bonds.

My shutter clicks cut through the rumble of conversations and laughter, each snapshot capturing a fragment of their essence. Brotherhood isn't just worn on patches, it is etched in every interaction, shared joke, and backslap.

"Hey, girl..." one member calls out, flexing his tattooed biceps for the camera, "... make sure you get my good side."

"Do you have a good side, Tank!" another mocks, and a round of chuckles ripples through the group.

I can't help but smile behind the viewfinder as I click away. Tattoos blur into leather, chrome glints under the sun, and all around me, the Royal Bastards wear their loyalty like armor.

Lucy told me there are a couple of chapters of the Royal Bastards here, and I feel perfectly safe.

Until I notice people diving for cover.

This is not men and women having fun and blowing off steam. In the distance, I see a man sprawled on the ground as blood oozes out of him. A bullet thuds into the man next to me. He buckles over and then falls to the ground. Turning, I look for cover and see Highway. He's running toward me, and I sprint for him. We collide as a bullet hits the dirt near us.

"Sniper," I say, looking up at the trees in the distance.

Highway puts my hand in his, and we run for cover behind a truck. Crouching down, I look at the chaos around us as MC members try to keep out of the snipers' sight.

"Stay here," orders Highway.

Reaching out, I grab his arm. "There are at least two snipers, and unless they're switching between weapons, there's also a handgun in the mix."

"How do you know?"

"Afghanistan taught me a lot. Do you have a spare gun?"

"On my bike."

"Well, what are we waiting for?" I grin at him, then jog to the next car.

The special forces soldiers taught me to keep low and never run in a straight line. A moving, unpredictable target is a lot harder to hit.

Chapter 2

HIGHWAY

Bullets thunk into the ground around me, but I barely notice them as I run for her. Gwen ducks behind a car, and if I didn't know better, I'd swear she was smiling. Her eyes lock with mine, and I hold out a hand, gesturing her to stay down and stay put. Another shot hits the ground at my feet, and I dive toward her.

"Stay the fuck down," I growl at her.

"Where's the fun in that?" She lifts her chin toward my bike. "Is the gun in your saddlebags?"

"You're going to get shot."

Gwen shakes her head. "Have you been listening to the shots and directions they're coming from?"

"I've been chasing you across the fucking field."

Her eyebrows shoot up in surprise. "That'll get you killed." Gwen turns and peeks over the top of the car we are hiding behind, her camera in her hand as she takes photograph after photograph. A bullet hits the car, and she ducks back down. "There's a shooter in the trees. He's in our direct line of sight, and if we go for your bike, we're as good as dead."

My gun is in my hand. I look down at it, but it doesn't have the range to hit the sniper in the trees.

"How many shooters?" I ask her.

"At least two. But the other one isn't firing. Our guy in the trees is providing cover for him to get away."

"You're *nothing* like your sister."

Gwen smiles, and it lights up her entire face. "Thanks for noticing." She frowns. "Hear that?"

"I don't hear anything."

"Exactly." She pokes her head up once more and looks across the field. "He's stopped shooting." I stand, and she grabs my hand and yanks down on it. "What the fuck are you doing?"

"You're right. He's stopped, which means he's dead or gone."

Gwen stands and hits me in the arm. "I could have been wrong!"

Grinning, I shake my head at her. "Something tells me, Gwen, there's not much you're wrong about."

Reaper jogs to stand near us. "You two okay?"

"Yeah." I nod.

"Boys are beating the bushes looking for the shooters," Reaper informs us.

"They're gone," states Gwen.

"We'll see," replies Reaper as he jogs away.

"I've gotta go." Gently, I put two fingers under her chin and tilt her head back. "Stay. Safe."

Gwen smiles. "Now, where's the fun in that?"

Bending, I press my lips to hers and then pull back an inch. "Here I was thinking Lucy was the wild one. But you, you're a whole different type of crazy."

The kiss sends a static charge through me as though the air is filled with electricity, almost like a magnetic pull.

"Nah, not crazy. Calculated risk taker. The shooter wasn't focused on us until everyone scattered." She holds up her camera. "And I got some crazy good shots."

"Find someone to take you back to town." My lips turn down. "Anyone but Justice." I press my lips to hers once more, then jog after Reaper.

Not waiting to see if Gwen obeys, my boots pound the gravel as I sprint toward Reaper, our VP, who is hovering over Creed. The president of the Royal Bastards MC is down, his white T-shirt soaked in crimson. Devil is there, her fingers white-knuckled, pressing hard against the gushing wound on Creed's shoulder.

"Stay with me, brother," Reaper growls, his voice

tight with command and barely concealed fear.

Creed bares his teeth and snarls, "It's a through and through. I'm fine."

"No, you're not," replies Devil, with a quiver in her voice.

My heart slams against my ribs. "We got you, Prez," I say, though it sounds more like a promise than reassurance.

"Highway!" The shout snaps my head around.

Damn. Gwen didn't listen. She's right behind me, her chest heaving, eyes wide but determined. There's no mistaking it—she's got guts. Fear is there, sure, but she's standing strong amidst the wailing chaos as if she belongs in this screwed-up world of ours.

"Should've known you wouldn't run," I mutter, half-annoyed, half-admiring.

"Not my style," she fires back, breathless.

My gut twists.

Protect her.

The thought slams into me with the force of a sledgehammer.

Seeing her there, fierce as hell, it ignites something—a need.

To guard.

To shield.

I can't let harm touch her, not if I have anything to say about it.

"Stick close," I tell her, my voice low. "This gets

worse... you're behind me. Got it?"

She nods, swallowing hard, and I feel the weight of her trust.

Devil's hands are slick and red, but her eyes are steel. She's a rock, even as Creed's face turns whiter than bone.

"Patch him up," Reaper barks and two of the guys tear open a med kit, their fingers clumsy with urgency.

I steal a glance at Gwen. She's pale, but her chin is lifted. Her eyes catch mine, and she holds my gaze. There's something fierce in her hazel eyes.

"Need help?" Her voice cuts through the tension, surprising me.

"Keep an eye out." It's all I can manage, my throat tight. But something passes between us, some current that zaps right through the tension.

"Got it." She nods, her lips pressing into a thin line and shifts slightly, angling her body toward the road.

Creed groans as someone presses gauze to his wound, a sound that punches me in the gut. "Hang in there, man."

"Like I got a choice," he grunts back, and there's a weak chuckle from the group that doesn't quite hide our shaking hands.

I look back at Gwen. The corner of her mouth quirks up just a fraction, but it's enough to stoke the fire that's been smoldering inside me since I first saw her.

"Thanks for staying," I say, the words rough like sandpaper.

"Where else would I be?"

"Good question." I smirk, but my heart's not in it. Too much is at stake. Too much blood on the ground.

She steps closer, her shoulder almost brushing mine. It's almost as if we're partners in this dance of danger, whether we choose it or not. And right now, I wouldn't have it any other way. We stand side by side, watching over our wounded president, over our brothers and sisters.

Surveying the crowd, Creed isn't the only one hit. I see at least five people being worked on and another sprawled out on the ground with his woman lying over him, crying.

Reaper locks eyes with me. "Find out who's hit."

Nodding, I move to walk away when sirens cut through the air, piercing and relentless. They're closing in fast. My gaze darts around, and my heart hammers against my ribs. I've tangled with the law enough times to know what comes next. Badges will swarm us with questions we aren't going answer.

"Someone wanted us hit," Gwen mutters, more to herself than to me, her brain ticking over like a well-oiled engine. "But who? And why?" She stares at the oncoming swarm of fast-approaching police cars.

"Questions for later," I tell her, but she's not content to sit back. I know Gwen will want to chase this rabbit down the hole.

Whoever came after my club, they've kicked a hornet's nest. They don't know the storm they've invited.

"Fine," Gwen concedes. "We will find out who's behind this." She looks up at me. "*Together.*"

Her lips press into a thin line, determination etched into every feature. We're knee-deep in chaos, our world turned upside down in a hail of bullets, but she's standing strong like she was made for this fight.

"Club business," I say as the sirens scream closer.

She's ready to dive headfirst into this madness with the club and me. Hell, maybe she's been waiting for something like this—waiting for a chance to prove she's more than just Lucy's kid sister.

Gwen holds up her camera. "I've got photographs. I can help."

I reach for the camera. She steps back and puts it behind her.

With a frown, I warn her, "Stick close," because somehow, in this screwed-up day, she's become mine to protect. "We'll go over the pictures together." I glance at the first police car that has come to a skidding halt. "And hide it from the cops." My hand finds hers, fingers intertwining naturally.

"Okay," she replies, her grip tight.

We're in this together—a biker and a beauty bound by blood and loyalty. What lies ahead will test us and push us to the brink. But as I look into Gwen's eyes, I know one thing is for sure—we're going to come out the other side. And when we do, nothing will ever break this bond we are forging.

Chapter 3

GWEN

The air feels thick with tension, and the field before me is a mess of tire marks, scattered debris, and blood. I stand there, fists clenched, heart pounding. Creed is on the ground, blood blooming across his chest and running down one arm. The gauze that covers it looks like a macabre flower.

I scan the chaos, my resolve steeling. Maybe this is why I'm here? I've been floating through life, trying to find my purpose for a while now. Perhaps if I find out who's gunning for the Royal Bastards and sell my story, I'll cement myself as a real reporter, or maybe I'll simply find a place to call home here with this club.

Blue and red lights flash, sirens wailing as the cops pour onto the field like ants.

"Step back!" one cop barks, his hand hovering

near his gun. Another kneels by Creed, his radio crackling with the urgency of life and death. "Dispatch, this is Officer Murphy. We have a gunshot victim at the Pumpkin Hill Creek Reserve. Requesting immediate medical assistance, please send an ambulance, over."

Questions fly hard and fast. "What happened here?"

"Who did this?"

The club members exchange glances. Silence hangs heavy, but survival trumps pride. For once, they are not at odds with the badges.

"Drive-by," Highway grumbles, his voice sounding like gravel mixed with frustration. "Didn't see who."

"Never saw it coming," Justice adds, his gaze locked on Creed's prone form.

"Unknown assailants," I offer, meeting the officer's probing eyes. There's no room for half-truths when blood is spilled.

"Stay put. We're gonna need to take your statements," the cop insists, flipping open a notebook.

As another officer approaches, it's evident he commands authority, and everyone instinctively clears a path for him. He leans over Creed, his expression turning to a frown when he scrutinizes him closely. Then, his gaze shifts, methodically meeting the eyes of each of us in turn.

"Is this a gang thing or a cartel thing?"

Reaper crosses his arms over his chest and looks the man up and down. "We don't know. We came out here to party. This isn't on us."

"Yeah, I saw your permit cross my desk. Didn't think you all would be stupid enough to open fire on each other."

Reaper's arms drop to his sides, and he leans forward, eyes blazing at the officer. "This *wasn't* us. We don't shoot our own."

The man glances down at Creed and drags one shoulder up to his ear. "Make no difference to me if you kill each other."

"Excuse me." I hold my camera up and snap a picture of the man. "Gwen Fullerton for *National Geographic*. I was out here doing a piece on the Royal Bastards. Am I to assume the Jacksonville PD isn't going to pursue those responsible, Officer..." I let my question hang there, waiting for this arrogant man to answer.

"*You* work for *National Geographic*?"

Reaching into my pocket, I pull out a card and hand it to him. He scans my business card, puts one hand on his hip, and makes a tut-tutting noise.

"Are you trying to tell me..." he waves my card around and grins at me, "... that you're not one of these club whores but a genuine reporter?"

"You can read, can't you?"

Highway's hand rubs the small of my back. I

know it's meant to calm me down, but this police officer is beyond rude.

Both hands go to his hips, and he leans forward. "I'm Sheriff Roy Baker. And just what is *National Geographic* doing with bikers?"

"I'm doing a piece about the urban rebel, the life of those who live outside the norm, of those who are free and unencumbered by the laws forced upon them by society." I smile warmly at the man, and he looks a little uncertain as the lies fall easily from my lips.

"You get any photos of this altercation?"

"No, sir. I had only just arrived and was scrambling for my life when the bullets went flying. You're welcome to check."

I hold out my camera to him, and Reaper's eyes widen. While he was talking to the sheriff, I sent the pictures of the day to the cloud and deleted them from my camera.

"Murphy," the Sheriff commands. "Escort this woman to your squad car and check her camera. If there's anything on it, secure it as evidence."

"You can't do that," I protest.

The sheriff looks me up and down. "Now, lady, you just watch me."

Officer Murphy places his hand on my elbow, and Highway steps toward him with a growl. His hand drops, and he points to a police car.

"Ma'am, if you'll come this way?"

Highway's eyes meet mine, and I place a hand on his chest. "I'll be right back."

He steps back and gives Officer Murphy a stare that makes the man swallow loudly. Despite the grim surroundings, a smile creases on my face. For a man who couldn't get himself to talk to me, Highway sure seems invested.

When we get to the squad car, I hold out my camera for Officer Murphy.

"Ma'am, if you could please just show me what's on it?"

"Sure. You're not good with technology?"

He shakes his head. "It's not that. I can see this probably cost you more than I make in a week, hell, maybe a month. I don't want to break it."

With a chuckle, I show him the photographs on my camera.

"You took pictures of the dirt?"

Nodding, I say, "When the gunfire started, I hit the ground and must have had my finger on the button." I shrug. "My usual gig is wildlife, not... this."

Officer Murphy places a hand on my upper arm. "You shouldn't be out here, ma'am."

"Please, call me Gwen."

Highway moves up behind Officer Murphy and clears his throat.

The officer immediately drops his hand and moves back. "Ahh, seems like the lady didn't get photos of anything important." The officer tips his hat at me. "Ma'am, I mean Gwen, we won't need to take your camera into evidence." He walks away, only glancing back at me once as he rejoins his boss near Creed.

"You know he's harmless."

Highway purses his lips together. "He's a cop."

"And that makes him trouble?"

"For the club, yes." Highway looks around. "I need to check on my people and want you to be safe. You know Winchester, yeah?"

"He's your sergeant at arms, right?"

"Find him. He'll be near someone who's injured or dead."

Reaching out, I place my hand on his chest and move closer to him. "Why can't I stay with you?"

"The police are going to keep us here. Winchester has a car. Ask him to borrow it." His hand covers mine. "Then go home. Stay there until I come for you." Highway bends at the knees to look me in the eyes and nods as though he needs me to do as I'm told.

"Okay." I look at our hands joined together on his chest. "But you'll find me later?"

"I said I would."

"No matter how late?"

He huffs out a laugh. "Yes, Gwen."

"Good." I slide my hand out from under his and search for Winchester.

The sergeant at arms stands apart from the fray,

a pillar of calm in a storm of panic and police tape. His eyes are sharp as he assesses the scene. They dart from cop to cop, reading them like a biker reads the road.

"Winchester," I call out, my voice slicing through the murmur of uneasy bikers.

He turns, his gaze locking onto mine. There's a flicker of surprise that he quickly masks beneath a stoic façade.

"Got a minute?" I ask, jerking my head toward the edge of the chaos.

He nods once, an almost imperceptible dip of his chin, and we move away from prying ears.

"Here's the deal," I start without a preamble. "Highway wants me to borrow your car and leave."

Winchester's jaw sets hard, his distrust for the badges around us almost tangible. I read caution in the lines of his face and see it in the way he gives nothing away.

"My car?"

"Yep. He seems to think law enforcement is going to keep you lot here for hours, but I'm just a journalist who saw nothing, so I should be let go."

Winchester raises an eyebrow. "You saw nothing?"

"Well, that's what they think." I hold up my camera.

He smirks. "It's a fucking mess. Are you going to the clubhouse?"

"Highway said to go home."

With a quick shake of his head, he says, "No. You're going to get those pictures printed and then come back to the clubhouse."

A tall, good-looking man with dirty-blond hair approaches us, blood dripping from his arm. "Winchester," he says by way of greeting, then fixes me with an intense stare.

"Ghost, this is Gwen. She's a reporter. Ghost is visiting from Iowa."

"Ahh, Lucy said there were other chapters here today. You're a long way from home," I say, meeting his piercing blue eyes.

He nods, his gaze shifting around. "Yeah, I thought the sun and sand would be good for me, but this? Nah, this is bad."

"It is," agrees Winchester with a nod. He points to Ghost's arm. "You got hit?"

"Just a graze." Ghost flexes his arm to inspect the wound, and I'm struck by how rugged and masculine he is.

"You should get it looked at. You don't want an infection," I say.

The two men exchange a glance before Ghost smiles at me. "I think I'll live." His eyes shift to the police cruisers in the distance. "How long before you think they'll let us leave?"

"Those with warrants will get pulled in, but the sooner we give them statements, the sooner we'll be out of here," replies Winchester.

"I've no desire to tangle with the law. One stint in jail is enough for me. Where's Creed?" Ghost asks.

Winchester looks around and shrugs. "No idea."

"You don't know? Oh, shit. Sorry."

Winchester straightens up. "Don't know what?"

"He got shot. He says it's a through and through, but they're working on him now."

Winchester's eyebrows shoot up in surprise. "Don't you think you should have led with that?"

"Sorry, I—"

"Where is he?" demands Winchester.

I point in the direction I came from. "Over there."

"How many are dead and injured?" asks Ghost.

"Three dead and six injured." He looks past me to a body in the field. "Whoever did this, they're not stopping. We need to find them first. Information is ammo," he says quietly.

"Exactly," I reply. "And right now, we're shooting blanks, but maybe I have something on film."

Winchester studies me, his eyes assessing, deciding if I can be trusted. Reaching into his jeans pocket, he pulls out a set of keys.

"It's the old red truck parked down there." He points toward his vehicle. "Make sure you clear it with the cops before you leave."

"Will do."

"I'll be seeing you, Lucy's sister."

"Gwen."

"I know." Winchester smirks then goes back to his MC brothers, and I head for Sheriff Roy Baker.

He's standing next to a couple of his men. The sheriff sees me coming, and his lips turn down in distaste.

"Excuse me, Sheriff?" He nods. "I was wondering if I could go?"

"Have you given a statement?"

"No, but—"

"Then no." The sheriff moves away from me with a dismissive flick of his hand.

Not wanting to be here any longer than I need to, I chase after him. "Well, perhaps I could ask you a few questions, Sheriff?"

He stops moving and turns to face me. "Questions?"

"Yes, sir. For instance, have the police got any suspects in the assassination attempt on the Royal Bastards?"

"Assassination attempt?" He rolls his eyes. "Seems more like the usual gun play between these fellas. You mark my words."

"Ahh, so the local PD already has a bias against the Royal Bastards and has jumped to conclusions without any evidence to back it up?"

Sheriff Roy Baker frowns. "You can go. Leave your name and address with Officer Murphy, and don't leave town."

"Can I get an official statement from you, Sheriff?"

"Not at this time. Now, go." He again waves a hand at me dismissively and walks away.

With a casual shrug, I stroll over to Winchester's old truck and hoist myself into the driver's seat. It protests with a coughing splutter as I turn the key, but soon, it settles into a smooth purr. As I drive away from the field, I glance in the rearview mirror.

There stands Highway, solitary, his gaze fixed on me as I depart.

It's so like him.

Observant.

Always watching.

Yet seemingly content with claiming little, if anything, for himself.

His distant demeanor is as deep as it is mysterious.

***

As I hop out of the truck, Dad greets me with a curious glance.

"New car?"

With a giggle, I shake my head. "Nah, borrowed it from one of the MC boys."

His lips turn down, and he stares at the old red beast. "She's definitely seen better days."

Slamming the door closed, I agree. "Maybe, but

she runs well." Dad has begrudgingly approved of Lucy and Reaper, but I'm not sure how he'll react to me being so close to an encounter with gun play, so I decide not to tell him about the sniper attack on the MC. I notice he has his briefcase in his grip, so instead, I ask, "Heading to work?"

"I have a meeting with one of the best plastic surgeon practices here in Jacksonville. I'm going to see if we're a good match for each other." Dad wraps me in a quick hug and plants a kiss on my cheek. "See you when I get back."

Holding up my camera, I say, "I'm going to develop these and then drop them off at the MC, so I might not be home."

"Okay, honey. Be safe." Dad climbs into his sleek silver Mercedes and drives away.

It's funny, when we lived in Miami, he would interrogate me about where I was going, but ever since we moved here, he's mellowed. I like to think it's because he trusts the MC to look after us more than he did his old circle of uptight friends.

Me telling him there was a gunfight wouldn't do either of us any good. The less Dad knows, the better, although he'll probably roast me for it later when it hits the news.

Walking into the house, I go downstairs to my workroom. Turning on my computer, I log into my cloud and download all the photographs I've taken, scrutinizing each one. The images aren't clear, but you can definitely make out faces, and maybe one of the MC brothers will recognize someone.

Clicking on all the images, I hit print and wait for the machine to give me hardcopies to take to the clubhouse.

***

I'm in the belly of the dimly lit clubhouse.

Most of the women are missing, and the men either look angry or defeated. The stench of spilled beer and old smoke hangs heavily in the air, a testament to countless nights of revelry, now overshadowed by the current mood. Winchester is leaning across a scarred table, his eyes lock onto mine, and a subtle lift of his chin serves as a greeting and an invitation to join him.

The clubhouse feels too quiet. My footsteps seem to echo as I walk across the room. Some of the men are drinking, but there's not a lot of conversation. It feels as though all eyes are on me as I sit opposite Winchester.

"Highway left a while ago to bring you here."

Glancing around the room, I put the A4 manila envelope on the table. "You told me to get these printed and get my ass back here."

His eyes flick to the envelope, then back to me. "Seems our road captain likes you. He said he told you to wait."

With a sigh, I say, "He did, but *you* told me to get these printed. Couldn't you have told him that?" Winchester shrugs. "How'd things go with the cops? Is Creed okay?"

A half-smile plays across Winchester's face. "They've kept a couple of us on outstanding warrants, but they'll be fine. As for Creed, he's a tough bastard. Although the way Devil is fussing over him, you'd think the man was on his deathbed." He gives the tabletop a couple of thoughtful taps. "We need to wait for Reaper before we look at your photos."

"Where is he?"

"With Highway on their way to get you."

Closing my eyes, I sigh. "Ahh, shit."

"Yep, that's about the size of it."

Pulling out my cell phone, I dial Highway.

His voice, rough as sandpaper, cuts through the silence, "Where the fuck are you?"

Cringing, I rush my words. "Sorry! I'm at the clubhouse. I printed the photographs and wanted to get them to you as soon as possible."

"You were told to wait."

His tone brings an involuntary roll of my eyes, causing Winchester to laugh. "Jesus, you and Winchester sound the same. I'm here."

Silence greets me on the other end of the line.

"Highway?"

"Yeah?"

"I'm sorry. I'll do as I'm told next time."

"You're damn straight you will."

The line goes dead, and I look at Winchester. "He's upset."

"He'll get over it." Winchester picks up his drink and swirls the liquid around in his glass. "Let's play a game. Memorize the faces in this room. Who comes, who goes."

I nod, taking mental snapshots of the MC. A burly man with a serpent tattoo strides in, and I commit his face to memory. A couple of men at the bar are standing together, whispering.

"If we weren't on friendly ground, I'd tell you to keep your back to the wall," Winchester continues, his gaze never wavering from the entrance. "Always see the exit. The key to not being seen is to blend in." He glances around the room. "For you, that would be jeans and a leather jacket. In this instance, it would be your camouflage."

"Why are you telling me this?"

Winchester ignores my comment and says, "Your eyes, they're your best weapon. Learn to listen with them."

"Listen with my eyes?" I question, skepticism edging my tone.

"See the twitch before the fist. The glance before the gun."

"Got it," I reply as I understand his meaning.

"Good." He gives a short nod, satisfied. "Now,

let's get you closer to the fire."

Standing, I pick up the envelope, and Winchester guides me through the clubhouse and out to a bonfire, his hand firm on my back. We sidle up to a group of brothers, close enough to eavesdrop, far enough to remain unseen.

"Observe their hands, their feet," he directs. "Details, Gwen. Details tell stories."

I hone in on a group in the corner, rough voices spilling tales of turf and trouble. My heart hammers as I soak up every word, every gesture.

"Who they fear, who they respect," Winchester murmurs, reading my focus. "It's all there if you know how to look."

"Like a game of chess," I say, catching on.

"Exactly," he confirms, a ghost of a smile touching his lips. "Remember, it's not just rival MCs or cartels. It's a world where every shadow could be an enemy."

"Or an ally," I counter, thinking of the alliances I've started to forge.

"True," he concedes, and there's a flicker of respect in his eyes. "You learn fast."

"Yo, Winchester!" Turning, a man and a woman are moving toward us. "How's Creed?"

"He's fine... it's not like he hasn't been shot before." Winchester points at me. "This is Gwen, she's Lucy's sister. Gwen, this is Dutch and Una from the UK."

Holding out my hand, Dutch shakes it firmly. "There are Royal Bastards in England?"

Una laughs. "They're everywhere."

"We were sent to oversee a couple of business deals." His eyes flick to Winchester. "But our business is done, so I'm thinking Una and I will head home as soon as we're able."

"Thought you two would want to hang around?" Winchester asks.

"We've been here for two weeks, and after this? It's time for us to get back to home soil." Dutch places a possessive tattooed arm around Una.

"Gun control in the UK is a hell of a lot better than here, right?"

Una winks at me. "Yes and no."

A car pulls up, and I watch Reaper and Highway hurry into the clubhouse. "We should get inside." Winchester holds out a hand to Dutch. "Don't leave yet. Give it a day or two just to be safe."

Dutch lets go of Una and shakes his hand. "As you wish."

Winchester nods solemnly and puts a hand on my elbow, guiding me back inside.

As the clubhouse door closes with a thud, the pungent odor of spilled beer overwhelms me. Winchester is at my side, his eyes scanning the room. I assume he is looking for his VP. First, I see Highway and then Reaper following close behind.

Holding up the envelope, I extend it to Reaper.

"These are for you."

Reaper looks me up and down, then takes it out of my hand. "Are you okay? When you weren't at home..." He glances at Highway. "Well, we were worried."

"Sorry, there was a communication breakdown." I give Winchester a sideways look. "And I thought you'd want these sooner rather than later."

Highway frowns. "We have no fucking idea who's gunning for us, and you decide to come here by yourself?"

Taken aback by his tone, I reply, "Yes, I did. Hell, you lot let me drive home *alone* in one of your MC's trucks. *If* someone was gunning for you *and* watching you, did it occur to you they may have followed me?"

Highway cocks his head to the side and stares at me, barely controlled anger rolling off him in waves.

"She has a point," chimes in Winchester.

Reaper holds up the envelope. "Enough." He slaps Winchester on the shoulder. "She's fine, and we have the photographs. Let's take a look."

The three men walk into a room, the one reserved for church. Aware of my status as an outsider, I'm conscious that entry is off-limits to me under normal circumstances.

Reaper turns and points at me. "Are you coming?"

His unexpected invitation momentarily throws me. Seizing the moment, I quicken my pace to join them, driven by curiosity and anticipation. The door swings open to reveal a large wooden table with the MC logo carved into its center. Chairs are arranged all around it, standing sentinel. My initial rush of excitement gives way to a hint of anticlimax. After all the secrecy and the strict boundaries set around this room, I had half-expected more. Something clandestine, perhaps. Yet here it stands, a simple meeting room.

"What?" asks Reaper as he stares at me.

With a quick smile, I reply, "Nothing."

He frowns and then sits at the head of the table with Highway and Winchester sitting on either side of him. Without saying a word, Highway pulls out the chair next to him, indicating I should sit there.

"Thank you," I say as I take my place at the table.

Reaper pulls out the photographs, stares at each one, hands them to Winchester, who passes them to Highway, and finally to me. No one speaks as they study the images before them. I'm waiting for the last picture. This one is the most blurry, but it is a close-up of one of the shooters.

"Fuck," mutters Reaper, his gaze fixed on the indistinct figure captured in the image before he tosses it to Winchester.

"Motherfuckers." Winchester's lips form a tight line as he slides it across the table to Highway.

"I'm sorry the image isn't clearer. I was hoping you might know who he is?"

Highway studies the photograph intently, then holds it out to me. "Not who specifically, but that tattoo on his wrist? It's the mark of the Crimson Wheelers MC."

"Is that good or bad?" I ask.

"Fucking bad," hisses Reaper. "We all know who's behind this now."

"Who?" I ask.

The men exchange silent glances, their reluctance to speak unsettling.

"Come on," I urge. "I risked my life to get these shots. At least give me the who and the why."

"Club business," Highway and Reaper say in unison.

Standing, I look down at Highway. "Well, fuck you too."

Winchester's laughter echoes behind me as I storm out of the room and through the clubhouse doors. I'm halfway across the compound when Highway catches up, his grip tight as he whirls me around to face him.

"What?" I reply with more force than intended.

He releases my arm. "Thank you for the photographs."

I scoff. "You chased me out of the clubhouse for that? To say thank you?"

Highway points at the clubhouse. "It's the way

we do things. You're not one of us."

Throwing my hands in the air, I turn once more and head for Winchester's truck. "Understood!"

Pulling the keys out of my pocket, I wrench open the door, but Highway's arm wraps around my waist, and he turns me around.

"What?"

He takes a deep breath and lets it out slowly. "The club appreciates you getting us those pictures." I roll my eyes and stare up at the sky. "Gwen, look at me."

Highway is far too close to me. Sucking in a deep breath, I lock eyes with him. "I get it... I'm a woman. If I had a penis, you'd share, but I don't. That's some deep male bullshit if I've ever heard it."

"That's got nothing to do with it." His eyes drop to my lips. "Even if you were a man, we wouldn't share. You're not a Bastard..." he pauses for a moment, then adds, "... and if you were a man, I wouldn't do this."

His hand moves up my back, he grips my ponytail as his other arm crushes me against him, and then Highway's lips find mine. In shock and totally unprepared, I let out a cry, and his tongue takes advantage, exploring my mouth.

At first, I press against his chest, trying to push him off, but as his lips meet mine with an intensity that ignites something primal within me, my resistance wanes. Tongues dance in a frenzy of desire, and his hand traces a path across my body, setting my nerves ablaze with each electrifying touch. My fingers claw at his T-shirt in a desperate bid to feel the warmth of the skin beneath.

Highway breaks the kiss, his eyes searching mine as his breaths come hard and fast. With a primal growl, he grabs my hand and yanks me across the compound, through the clubhouse, and up a flight of stairs. He walks down a hallway, opens a door, pulls me inside, and slams it shut behind us. Before I can even comprehend our surroundings or the whirlwind of events unfolding, his lips capture mine again.

This all feels way too fast. I'm not this woman. I don't sleep with someone until I know them.

Highway runs his chin up my neck—*maybe I am this woman.*

Clumsy fingers move to his belt as I struggle to undo it while his hands explore my body, and I find myself pressing against him, desperate for more. Highway pulls my shirt up over my head and removes his own, exposing all his tattoos. He roughly yanks down my bra, and his mouth captures one of my nipples. I cry out as his tongue flicks across its sensitive surface.

Holding him there as he sucks and teases me, my thighs feel like they are on fire, and I moan out in frustration when he stops.

Highway drops to his knees. "Sit," he orders.

Not wanting this to stop, I do as he demands. Highway removes my boots and pushes me back on the bed. His fingers undo my belt, and he pulls my jeans and underwear down my legs. I'm bare in front of him but feel no embarrassment or self-consciousness—he makes me feel sexy.

Scooting up the bed, Highway watches me, takes off his belt, kicks off his boots, and undoes the top button of his jeans. With a predatory smile, Highway crawls up the bed. He blows on my pussy, sending a shiver through me. He smiles as he moves farther up my body, where his lips meet mine as he lowers himself over me. At first, I'm frustrated he's not naked, but the feel of denim against my pussy is exciting. I spread my legs further and wrap them around his waist as we kiss, grinding into him with abandon.

Reaching between us, Highway touches my clit, and I arch into him, desperately wanting more. With deft fingers, he teases me, bringing me to the edge and back many times.

"Please, I need more," I beg.

"Will you do as you're told?"

His question surprises me, and I look at him, confused. "What do you mean?"

Highway smiles. He moves down my body, his tongue going between my folds, where he licks and sucks. The orgasm is almost upon me. This man knows what he's doing—I'm about to shatter into a million pieces. With both hands wrapped in his hair, I spread my legs wider, holding him in place.

Highways stops and sits back on bended knees. "Will you do as you're told?" he asks once more as his fingers move in and out of me.

This time, there's no hesitation. I nod as his thumb applies pressure to my clit, and all rational thought leaves me.

"Say it," he demands.

"Yes."

Highway stands and lets his jeans fall to the floor. He's perfect. All muscle, tattoos, and a huge cock which is hard and glistening on its tip.

"Will you do as you're told?" he asks again.

"Yes, I'll do as I'm told."

A smile spreads across his face as he strokes himself up and down. "Good girl."

He bends and kisses from my knee to my pussy, where he brings me once again to the brink. This time, he doesn't stop, and my orgasm washes through me. I then feel him push his way inside as his thumb applies pressure to my clit. The waves of ecstasy keep coming as he pounds into me.

"So. Fucking. Tight." Highway grunts. "And now you're *mine*."

I'm on fire as he fucks me. His huge cock hits the right spot with every thrust. Every kiss and grunt intensifies the sensations sweeping through me. Our bodies are slick with sweat as we move in unison. Highway pulls out, stands, grabs my ankles, drags me down the bed, and then flips me over.

"On your knees."

I do as I'm told and go up on all fours. Slowly, he pushes himself inside me, then just as slowly, he pulls out. Highway then moves faster, and my arms shake as he goes deeper.

"Yes," I cry out.

"Harder?"

"Yes!"

Highway's cock keeps hitting me just right. I need to move and find another release.

Rocking back, I match his pace. The sound of our bodies colliding and the occasional grunt fills the room. My orgasm courses through my veins, and I come so hard I cry out his name.

"Good girl," he growls.

Highway thrusts inside me one last time as his seed fills me.

We are locked together. My body is a quivering mess, and when he pulls out of me, I cry out. Overwhelmed, a sob escapes me and then another. My arms and legs are locked in place, unable to move. Tears course down my cheeks as I try to control my emotions and this feeling of finding my perfect mate. It's then that something warm touches my pussy and ass. He's cleaning me with a washcloth.

"It's okay," he whispers. "Sometimes it can feel

very intense."

I nod, unable to do anything else.

Highway lies on the bed and drags me up so I'm lying on his chest. His fingers stroke my hair and back as I lay there, not moving or speaking.

Exhausted and sated, I fall asleep in his arms, feeling protected, cared for, and well and truly fucked.

Chapter 4

HIGHWAY

Gwen's breathing is even as she sleeps with her head on my chest. Today hasn't gone at all the way I thought it would. The day started with me wondering if I could get her to have a drink with me, and now she's in my bed. Little does she know, but Gwen Fullerton is mine. There will be no date with Justice. If she still wants to go to the swamp, I'll take her. A smile creeps across my face—Justice is going to be pissed when he knows I've beaten him.

A soft knock sounds on my door, and Devil sticks her head inside. "You're wanted." She shuts the door, and I try to scoot out from under Gwen.

"Are you doing a hit and run?"

Sitting up, I shake my head. "No. Club business." Gwen sits up and reaches for her clothes. "You don't have to go. Stay. Maybe we can continue this later?"

"I'm not." She puts on her bra. "I'm coming with you."

"It's not how we do things." Standing, I pull on my jeans and then a T-shirt.

Gwen is silent as she dresses, and then she puts her hands on her hips and stares at me.

"What?"

"What?" She throws her hands in the air. "*What?*" Gwen shakes her head, holds up a hand, and thumps her chest. "If it weren't for me, you wouldn't even know who shot your president."

"We are grateful for your help."

"Pfft!" Gwen spins around, throws the door open, and strides down the hallway, leaving me behind.

"Gwen!"

"It's fine!"

Fine is the universal word from a woman when everything is far from *fine* as you can get. Gwen is a spitfire, and watching her walk away should probably piss me off, but a part of me thinks it's as hot as hell. Reaching for her, I wrap my hand around her upper arm and spin her around.

"Stop," I say quietly, but with a small amount of steel in my voice. She opens her mouth to speak, and I place a finger over her lips. "If I'm allowed, I'll share what I find out, but you are not a brother, not one of us. We do things a certain way. It's not only for our protection but also for those we care about.

So stop being all pissy and give me a break."

"You care about me?"

"I said all that, and all you heard was that I care about you?"

Gwen's eyes drop to my chest. "Maybe."

Stepping back, I crouch down a little to look her in the eyes. "I've gotta go. Can we talk about this later?"

Gwen nods. "I'm still mad."

With a smirk, I kiss her and say, "I know."

Gwen follows me down the stairs, but when I move into the clubhouse meeting room, she keeps going outside without a backward glance.

Sitting at the table is Creed. He's pale, and Devil is beside him.

He sucks in a breath and gives me a chin lift. "She looked pissed."

"Women," I reply and sit down.

"Pfft!" huffs out Devil. "I'm guessing by the look on her face just now that *you* did something wrong."

Creed holds up a hand. "Babe, can you give us the room?"

Devil nods once, kisses his cheek, and leaves.

Creed waits until the door is closed before he speaks, "What do we know?"

"It was the Crimson Wheelers MC," states Reaper.

"So that means the Khans are looking to expand." Creed sucks in a breath and holds a hand to his shoulder. "Fuck it all to hell."

Reaper nods. "Yeah, we need to strike back."

Creed nods, then looks at Winchester. "Set up a meet. Somewhere neutral."

Reaper shakes his head several times. "A meet? Fuck that, they need to bleed."

Creed holds up a hand. "*If* they are behind this, they will." He locks eyes with Winchester. "Set up the meet... take Highway with you." With effort, Creed stands, then places a hand on Reaper's shoulder. "Cooler heads need to prevail, and I need you to make sure we don't go off half-cocked. I need you, brother, to look after things. To make sure our men and club are safe and protected."

"We need a show of force," snarls Reaper.

Creed takes a deep breath and slowly exhales. "Reaper, I'm asking you to wait. Do you honestly think I don't want someone to bleed? A war with the Khans will disrupt all our supply chains."

Reaper stands and faces Creed. "So, money over brotherhood?"

"For fuck's sake, Reaper, that's not what he's saying. The smart move is to confirm who's behind this, and then we make them bleed." I slam my hand on the table, the noise echoing through the room.

"Thanks, Highway." Creed nods at me and shuffles toward the door. "Reaper, once we confirm it's the Khans, the streets of Jacksonville will run red with their blood, but in case it's not them but someone who will profit from a war, I want confirmation."

Reaper casts me a glance. "Is there something I don't know?"

"We will see," replies Creed, then he moves toward the door. Devil opens it and immediately puts her arm around Creed's waist. "I'm fine."

She smiles up at him. "I know. But it's not every day your husband gets shot, so you need to put up with me fussing for a bit. Let's get you to bed."

Creed smiles and winks at me. "This one's always trying to get me into the sack."

"Yeah, yeah, that's me." Devil doesn't look at anyone as she walks with Creed down the hallway and disappears into their room.

"Why's he out of the hospital?" I look at Winchester.

He shrugs. "Because he's a tough bastard."

"And I promised Devil I'd have medical here to take care of him," says Reaper. "Need you two to carry out his orders. Let me know when and where."

"You're doing as he says?" I ask incredulously.

Reaper fixes me with a look. "Until he's dead and buried, he's our president, and I do as I'm told." He slaps me on the shoulder and walks away.

"Something tells me Reaper does what Reaper wants."

Winchester shrugs. "Reaper will keep it locked

down until we prove the Khans went after us, then God help them. Come on, we've got shit to do."

He pulls his cell phone out of his pocket and heads for the door. Following close behind, I listen as he puts his phone to his ear.

"Anthony, it's Winchester. We need a meet." He throws a leg over his bike. "How about now... you, me, and one of our boys?" He nods. "Yeah, bring whoever you want." Winchester grins at me. "You know we own that club?" He pauses as he listens. "Okay, cool. See you in a bit. I'll call ahead, so we've got the VIP room."

"Is it weird they picked one of our clubs?"

Winchester tilts his head from side to side. "If you're asking me *if* they did it? No idea. But the fact he's not worried and wants to meet at one of our clubs either means they don't think we can trace it back to them or they didn't do it. Let's find out."

Chapter 5

GWEN

Sitting in Winchester's truck, the key is cold and heavy in my hand. It fits snugly into the ignition, but I don't turn it. Instead, I'm parked here, wrestling with my thoughts, my gaze locked on the clubhouse's entrance. I'm desperate for Highway to step out and beckon me into his secretive world.

As if on cue, the door swings open, and there they are, Highway and Winchester, deep in conversation as they stride toward their bikes. My heart sinks a bit. It's clear Highway prefers to keep me out of the club's inner workings. Yet, nobody ever said I couldn't keep a watchful eye from afar. With a smirk, I fire up the engine and pull out, trailing them at a safe distance.

The neon lights of a strip club soon come into view. I'm sure they would cast a lurid red shadow across the pavement at night, but they look tacky in the harsh light of the day. The sign, a seductive outline of a woman, flickers intermittently. I park up the street close enough to keep them in sight. The bouncer greets them with hearty laughter, a camaraderie I can almost feel from my vantage point. My camera lens catches the moment, snap after snap—the casual exchange, the unguarded smiles.

A few more patrons slip inside, nondescript and hardly worth a second glance. But then, three suited men arrive, their demeanor setting off silent alarms in my mind. There's a confidence in their stride, a rehearsed casualness. They parade in front of the bouncer, jackets open, a slow pirouette to show they're unarmed. Unimpressed, the bouncer blocks their path with a raised hand and murmurs into his walkie-talkie. Denied entry initially, they linger until a woman, all charm and smiles, appears and ushers them inside with a practiced grace.

As the day drags on, I keep my lens busy, capturing the comings, goings, and fleeting exchanges. Hours later, Winchester, Highway, and the suited trio emerge. Their laughter spills into the air, easy and genuine. They shake hands and point at some shared joke, their camaraderie thick. Then, as quickly as they had arrived, Highway and Winchester roar off on their bikes, leaving with a final wave to them.

The three men linger until the bikes are mere echoes in the distance. Then, with a signal, a sleek black Escalade glides to the curb. They slip inside with a final scan of the quiet street, and I start the truck and follow them.

They weave in and out of the traffic, and I try to keep my distance. Eventually, they turn into a driveway bordered by imposing six-foot fences—a fortress of solitude deep in the countryside. As I drive past, one of the men steps out of the Escalade, his hand covertly slipping under his jacket.

Shit.

I've been made.

My foot slams down on the accelerator, the engine roaring in protest as I speed away. I glance anxiously in the rearview mirror. Thankfully, no one appears to be in pursuit. Once I'm sure I've lost them, I ease off the gas. Jacksonville's back roads are a maze to my unfamiliar eyes. I pull over to the side of the road, the gravel crunching under the tires, and grab my cell phone to pull up Google Maps, squinting at the screen as I try to orient myself and plan my next move.

A knock sounds on my window, and I jump, dropping my cell phone on the truck's floor.

"Hey, darlin'," a man in a black suit drawls from the other side of the closed window. "Playing with the big boys now?"

"I'm lost," I reply, trying to keep my voice steady.

"Listen, sweetheart," he grunts as he taps the window. "The boss would like to talk to you."

"I'm good," I retort, my chin held high.

His lips twitch in a smirk that doesn't reach his cold eyes. He shakes his head and chuckles, dark and menacing. "Doesn't work that way." A car pulls up in front of the old truck. "You can either follow us, or we can help you into the car. Your choice."

"I'll follow."

He chuckles once more, nods, then strolls back to the car parked behind me. I lean over, my fingers brushing against the cold, familiar plastic of my cell phone as I pluck it from the floor. Hastily, I dial my sister while shifting the truck into drive, turning around to tail them back toward the estate.

"Hey, Gwen, what's up?" Lucy mumbles, her voice heavy with sleep.

"Sorry, Sis, but is Reaper there?" I ask, ignoring her grogginess.

"Are you okay?" she responds, her voice sharpening with concern.

"Yes," I answer, but my pitch is a tad too high, the waver in my tone betraying my nervousness.

There's a moment of muffled talking on the other end.

"Gwen?" It's a deeper voice this time—Reaper's.

"Reaper, I may have fucked up," I confess, gripping the steering wheel tighter.

"Where are you?" His voice is calm but edged

with urgency.

"I have no idea, but I'm being escorted to an estate on the outskirts of Jacksonville. It has large fences, and the number on the gate is 1515."

"Who is doing the escorting?"

I hesitate, my stomach twisting. "Don't be mad. But I followed Highway and Winchester to a strip club where they met these guys, and now…" My voice trails off, leaving the gravity of the situation to hang in the air.

"Fucking hell." He exhales sharply, the line crackling with his frustration.

As the gates to the estate swing open, I follow the car until it stops in front of an imposing mansion. Armed men patrol the grounds with an unsettling ease, their eyes scanning the area, yet none spare me even a fleeting glance. The same man who approached me on the roadside taps on my window, motioning for me to get out.

"I've gotta go," I murmur into the phone.

"Wait!" Reaper's voice barks from the other end. "Give the phone to someone in charge and do it now."

Obediently, I wind down the window and hand the phone to the man. "He wants to talk to you," I tell him.

With a reluctant sigh, he takes the cell phone from my hand and presses it to his ear. "Yes?" He steps away, pacing as he talks to Reaper, nodding several times. "She's a reporter?" he says into the phone, then his gaze snaps to mine, assessing. "Boss wants to meet her." He shakes his head in response to whatever Reaper is saying on the other end. "No can do. The boss wants a meet, so she gets to meet him." He ends the call and hands me back my phone with a terse, "Let's go, princess."

He opens my door, and I slide out, standing awkwardly on the paved driveway.

"You don't look like a club whore," he remarks offhandedly.

"And what does a club whore look like?" I retort, my curiosity piqued despite the tension.

"Not like you." He gestures toward the mansion. "Go inside, turn left, and take a seat in the study. Someone will be with you soon."

Driven by habit, I clutch my camera a little tighter to my side and follow his instructions, stepping into the mansion's cool, shadowy interior. My heart races as I navigate through the luxurious yet foreboding space. The moment I step into the room, the sheer size of the wooden desk commands attention while the chair positioned behind it seems pulled straight from a set designer's dream, its ornate design reminiscent of scenes from a James Bond film. In stark contrast, the guest seat, crafted from the same material, appears almost humble in size.

Raising my camera, I capture the scene before

me and swiftly upload the images to the cloud. A soft sound interrupts my focus, and I turn to find a man standing before me, a warm smile gracing his lips.

"Please, take a seat," he gestures gracefully.

As he settles into his oversized throne-like chair, a grin tugs at my lips at the comical sight of him, engulfed by its grandeur.

"What's amusing?" he asks, his brow furrowing slightly.

Unable to contain my amusement, a laugh escapes me. "Isn't it a bit... extravagant?" I remark, motioning toward the elaborate chair. "You look rather... theatrical."

His expression darkens. "Why were you trailing my associates?"

"I wasn't," I protest, my voice tinged with earnestness. "I'm new in Jacksonville, simply finding my bearings."

"A likely story," he retorts, skepticism evident in his tone. "Do you often consort with bikers?"

"I told you, I'm still settling in," I explain, my words tinged with exasperation. "Trying to build connections."

"Yet you find yourself tailing members of the Royal Bastards," he observes sharply. "We may be friendly with certain circles, but you... you're an unknown entity."

I clutch my camera with a sense of urgency,

hoping its presence will lend credibility to my explanation. "I'm a journalist," I reveal, my voice steady. "I've been researching a piece on the Royal Bastards. When your men met with them at the strip club, I saw an opportunity to delve deeper into the story."

"So, you admit to trailing my associates?" he presses, his gaze unwavering.

"Yes," I concede, meeting his gaze with resolve. "In pursuit of the truth."

"Pursuit of what truth, exactly?"

Shifting uneasily in my seat, I clear my throat before speaking, "There's been a declaration of war against them, an attempt on their president's life, and a few of their members have been killed. I thought perhaps when they met with your men, there might be some sort of involvement."

He rises from his chair, a fluid motion that exudes authority, and circles around the desk, extending his hand expectantly for my camera. With a sense of reluctance, I surrender it to him. He deftly navigates its controls, scrutinizing the footage with a furrowed brow before returning it to me.

"We had no part in those events. None whatsoever. Do you understand?"

"Then why the rendezvous with the Royal Bastards?" I press, unable to shake my curiosity.

"This ..." he gestures between us, his demeanor

resolute, "... is not an interview. You will delete your pictures." He looks over my head and nods at someone. Turning, I see the back of a man as he walks away. "It seems the Royal Bastards like you. Two of them are at my gates."

"Only two?"

He barks out a laugh. "You were expecting more?"

"Hoping, more like it."

"Delete the pictures. Now," he commands as he retreats behind the enormous desk. "And then you can be on your way."

Having already uploaded to the cloud, I do as he says and stand. "Who are you?"

"I'm a businessman, nothing more." He smiles widely at me. "And, Miss Fullerton, the next time you decide to chase a story, it better not have anything to do with me." He waves a hand at me dismissively. "You may go."

Not needing to be told twice, I hustle out to the truck, where a man holds open the door, and as I slide into it, he takes my camera.

"Hey!"

He gives me a bored look as he flicks through my photographs, then hands it back. "Have a nice day."

Turning over the ignition, the truck roars to life, and I speed down the driveway and onto the street where Highway and Winchester are waiting.

Highway motions for me to wind down my

window. "Follow us." His tone and expression tell me all I need to know.

He's pissed.

Chapter 6

HIGHWAY

The meeting with the Khans has cleared them of involvement in the rally shooting, but Gwen's unauthorized surveillance jeopardizes our relationship with them. Reaper's anger over the phone was palpable, and I'm seething too.

Gwen, headstrong and willful, has a knack for getting under my skin. Despite the excitement she brings, she needs to learn our ways and understand the boundaries we uphold.

As we pull into the compound, Reaper waits outside the clubhouse, a silent sentinel of authority. His subtle gesture of a chin lift calls me to him. Winchester and I dismount, striding across the compound with purpose, ascending the stairs in unison.

"Winchester, meet us inside," Reaper directs,

and Winchester acknowledges with a nod before continuing on his path. Reaper's hand rests on my chest as he halts me. His question catches me off guard. "Do you like this woman?"

"W-what?" I stammer, taken aback by the sudden inquiry.

"Do you like her?" His gaze pierces through me, demanding honesty.

"Yes," I admit without hesitation.

"If you're keeping her, you need to let her in," he asserts, his words weighted. It's a departure from our club's strict code of secrecy, a breach of tradition that leaves me unsettled. "Not everything, but enough. Lucy has my back. If you believe Gwen has yours, then she deserves to know, but..." he pauses, his gaze drifting to Gwen, "... make it clear she can't breathe a word of it. Understand?"

"No," I respond, uncertain of the implications.

"Then figure it out," he commands, his tone final. His attention shifts to Gwen. "You. Inside. Now."

Turning, I look at Gwen. She's clutching her camera to her chest and looks apprehensive.

Good.

She *should* be worried.

Hell, she could have gotten herself killed.

Reaper casts one final glance in our direction before striding back into the clubhouse, disappearing into the confines of our meeting room.

"How worried should I be?" Gwen's voice breaks the silence, laden with uncertainty.

Pursing my lips in a hard line, I look into her eyes. "You fucked up. But you're a big girl, right?"

"You shut me out. What was I supposed to do?"

"Maybe, trust me?"

Turning, I walk inside and take my place at the table. Gwen steps into our meeting room, and Reaper shuts the door.

"What were you thinking?" Reaper's voice cuts through the tension as he strides around the table, taking his place at its head.

Gwen, undeterred, places a hand on her hip. "Let's be clear, *you* shut me out. I was simply following a lead."

"By trailing me and Winchester?" my tone bristles with frustration. "Did it even occur to that pretty, pampered brain of yours that you could have been in danger? Why do you think we met with the Khans? For our health?"

Gwen throws her hands in the air. "Oh, shut it! I came to you with evidence, and you all shut me down. What did you want me to do? Sit at home like a good little woman and do nothing?"

I rise from my seat so abruptly that it slams against the wall. "No, I expected you to trust *me* and let the MC handle it," I retort, my voice echoing with frustration.

"That'll do," Reaper interjects, his authoritative

tone halting our exchange. We both turn our attention to him. "What did you hope to accomplish by tailing Winchester and Highway?"

"To find out who went after the MC."

"And why do you care?"

Gwen glances at me. "My sister is in this life." She turns to face Reaper. "You're her partner. The MC has been good to me and my dad." Gwen sighs. "I only wanted to help." Her voice has dropped to a whisper.

"You were lucky. The Khans could have made you disappear without a trace."

"I'm—"

"Now's not the time for you to speak." Reaper stands. "Winchester, give her a crash course on how not to be seen."

Winchester nods. "I can do that."

"Highway, make sure she stays out of trouble. And Gwen, you don't ever go off on your own again. When we tell you it's club business, you keep out of it. Are we clear?"

"Y-yes."

"Good. Now, I've got to debrief Creed." Reaper leaves the room.

Gwen is the first to speak. "What just happened?"

"I think Reaper knows your sister and knows you won't go away quietly. Come on, I'll show you how to blend." Winchester stands. "Unless you'd rather he handed you over to the Khans?"

"No, no, no. He was scary."

"You haven't seen scary," I state as I stalk out of the room.

"What's that supposed to mean?" Gwen asks as she grabs my arm.

"Oh, princess, you're going to learn what that means later."

Winchester laughs, and Gwen lets go of my arm and steps back. I give her a once-over, then walk up the stairs to my room.

Women in this life do as they are told, and no matter what Reaper has to say, Gwen will do as *I* say.

Chapter 7

WINCHESTER
Sergeant at Arms

There is a dive bar on the edge of town, the kind of place that reeks of trouble. It's where I'm introducing Gwen to the shadier parts of the MC life.

"Act natural," I whisper to her as we sidle up to the bar.

Gwen is dressed in jeans and a black tank top, her hair is down, and she looks like any other female here. I'm not wearing my colors, so I can blend in with the locals.

"Whiskey, neat." I hold up two fingers and smile at Gwen.

The bartender puts one in front of each of us. The amber liquid burns going down. Gwen almost chokes on hers, and I smirk at her.

"First time here?" A biker with tattoos crawling up his neck, colors I don't recognize, asks Gwen.

"Passing through," she says in a casual tone.

"Careful." He grins at her, revealing yellowed teeth. "This ain't a place for tourists."

"Thanks for the tip," Gwen replies.

"Who you with?" he asks.

"Nobody important." Gwen shrugs.

"Let's take a walk," he suggests, or rather, demands, and lays a hand on her shoulder.

Gwen's eyes go wide, but before I can react, another figure steps up, sliding between them with a dangerous ease.

"Back off, she's with me," Justice growls, an arm wrapping protectively around her waist.

"Is that right?" the biker sneers, eyeing Justice's cut, the Royal Bastards' insignia emblazoned across it.

"Problem?" Justice challenges, his stance ready for a fight.

"None at all," the biker backs off, his smile twisting into a snarl. "Just making friends."

"Let's go," Justice murmurs, steering Gwen toward the door with a firm grip.

I follow them out at a distance.

Once outside, Justice breathes deep, tension bleeding from his shoulders. "You good?"

"Better now," Gwen admits. "Did Reaper send you?"

"No, but I can't let you have all the fun," he quips, but there's an edge to his voice, something protective. "Or get yourself killed."

"I had it under control."

Justice looks at me and nods. "It appeared as though she was in over her head. I was only trying to help."

"It was a test... one she failed."

"Wait! What?"

Sighing, I say, "What would you have done to get away from that man?"

"I thought you'd step in."

"And if I didn't?"

Anger flashes across her features. "You know I can take care of myself."

Justice chuckles. "And it wasn't Reaper who sent me but Highway."

Gwen looks stunned at his revelation. "Really?" He nods. "Thanks."

"Anytime," he replies.

The ride back to the compound is done in silence. Gwen stares out the window, chewing on her bottom lip. When we come to a stop, and I turn off the engine, Gwen reaches over and touches my arm.

"How was I supposed to handle it?"

"You should have told him you were there with me, and he would have backed off."

Feral is walking across the compound, head

bowed, putting one foot in front of the other, not paying attention to those around him. "See him? That's Feral. He's scary as fuck to most of the females. About this time, he goes to a bar down by the beach. Get Justice to take you. See how you go up against a real animal."

Chapter 8

GWEN

The dive bar looms ahead, a neon sign flickering like a beacon of bad decisions. It's the kind of place nice girls don't visit. I kill the engine and slide out of the truck. A Harley pulls up beside me, and it is Justice.

"Watch yourself," Justice warns, eyes scanning for trouble.

"Always do," I shoot back with a wink. I'm nervous, sure. But I can't let that show.

The door groans, protesting my entrance. Inside, it's a haze of cigarette smoke and desperation. I spot Feral immediately and stroll over to stand near him.

"Hey, doll." He leers, his gaze crawling over me.

I resist the urge to scrub at my skin.

"You're Feral?" I slide onto the stool beside him.

"I need info."

He chuckles like I've told a good joke and takes a swig of his beer. "And what's in it for me?"

"Knowing you helped keep your ass safe," I retort.

His eyes narrow as if he's considering, weighing his sleazy desires against self-preservation.

"Fine. What do you wanna know?" He leans in, his breath reeking of alcohol and neglect.

"Who ordered the hit on your brothers?"

Feral runs a hand through greasy locks, thinking. "That's the million-dollar question."

"Do you know?" I press, my voice low, urgent.

"Maybe." He grins, a smile full of malice and bad intentions. "Could be for a little somethin' somethin', I might get talkative."

"Thanks, Feral," I say, sliding off the stool. "But I'm not interested in that with you." His hand snakes out, catching my wrist.

"Be careful, Gwen," he says, and there's a glimmer of something almost like concern in his bloodshot eyes.

"Always am," I reply, yanking free.

He laughs, and I tilt my head to the side. "How do you know my name?"

Winchester comes out of the shadows. "You blew it, Feral."

"Shit. Sorry, man." Feral dips his chin and walks away from us.

"This was another test?"

"Yeah, you did better this time." He points a thumb over his shoulder at Feral. "Although he would do anything for a bit of skin on skin. You never know what you might have learned."

A shiver runs up my spine, and I shake my head. "He doesn't know anything. He was only looking to get laid."

"How did you know?"

"He's one of you. He wears the cut. His loyalty isn't in question."

Winchester nods. "Yeah, but someone ratted us out." I frown at him. "One of the men who was hit was standing in front of me. They were trying to take out the leadership."

"And they nearly succeeded with Creed."

"Yep." Winchester picks up a beer bottle and takes a sip.

"Yeah, but it wasn't one of the Royal Bastards... maybe someone within your circle but not one of you."

Winchester looks thoughtful and taps his chin. "Yeah, I thought that too."

Justice stands next to me. "What are you two up to?"

"Come on, let's take a ride. See who's getting a shipment down by the docks." Winchester smiles. "You can ride with Highway."

"He's here?"

"Yeah, you didn't check your surroundings." Winchester nods to a lone figure in the corner of the bar.

Shit, I didn't even look to see if there were any threats in the bar.

Some investigative journalist I am.

Highway stands and crosses the room. One side of his mouth kicks up, but he looks anything but pleased to see me.

"Gwen's with you. We're going to check out the docks. If this is what we think it is, maybe they'll show their hand."

"We're supposed to have a pickup tonight?" asks Highway.

"Yeah, but with everything that's happened, Creed had me move the pickup, but only he and I know that. If someone was after our shipment, maybe they thought taking us out would make it easy pickings."

Highway crosses his arms across his chest. "And you're only telling us this now?"

Winchester chuckles. "Need to know, and you didn't need to know, but now you do." He raises his chin at Justice. "You got the walkies and binoculars?"

"Yeah, I do."

"Let's roll then."

***

The darkness envelops us like a thick cloak as we hunker down outside the warehouse. I'm pressed against the cold, unforgiving metal of a shipping container, the stench of rust and decay thick in my nostrils. Highway crouches beside me, all coiled power and dark intensity. His presence is both a comfort and a spark in the tinderbox of my adrenaline.

"Movement," Winchester murmurs into the comms, his voice a ghost in the static.

I peer through the binoculars, catching sight of shadowy figures moving crates with methodical haste. They're oblivious to our watchful eyes, cockroaches scuttling in the open unaware.

"Got it," Justice confirms from his perch high above on a decrepit fire escape. His silhouette merges with the darkness.

"Fuckers," Feral spits beside me, his disdain palpable even in the scant light. "They think they can steal from us?"

"Focus," I snap, my finger itching on my camera's trigger. "Need clear shots." Click after click, I document their sins.

"Easy there, ace," Highway whispers, his voice a low rumble that vibrates through my bones. He reaches out, steadying my hand.

"Thanks," I breathe out, surprised by the flutter in my chest. It's ridiculous—this isn't the time for whatever electric current is arcing between us. But damn, if it doesn't make me feel alive.

"Anytime," he replies, a corner of his mouth lifting in a half-smile that's all danger and promise.

We sit in silence, watching them load crates into the backs of several trucks.

"Who are they?" I ask.

Highway glances at Winchester, who nods. "Crimson Wheelers MC. They're new to Jacksonville."

"No, they fucking ain't. They've been here for a year," loud whispers Feral. "Creed said we should have moved them on, and now look at what they've done."

Highway scowls at him. "They're big in New Orleans. Lately, they've been expanding."

My gaze drifts back to the MC members, oblivious to their impending downfall, a spiderweb of deceit they can't see. And the Royal Bastards are the spiders, patient and deadly.

"Got enough?" Highway asks, his hand resting lightly on my back, grounding me.

"Enough to bury them," I confirm, feeling the weight of responsibility tighten around my shoulders.

"Then let's get the hell out of here."

We fade back into the shadows, a seamless retreat. There's work to do, a club to protect, and my personal feelings have to wait.

"Good work tonight," Highway says once we're a

safe distance away, his gaze meeting mine in the moonlight. "But next time you want answers, you ask me. You don't go off on your own."

"I'm really sorry. It's just you all have this man code, and I didn't think you'd share anything with me, but I can help. Hell, I have helped." I hold up the camera. "These images again prove it's the Crimson Wheelers. But who is giving them the orders?"

"If it's not the Khans, that only leaves one other cartel who would oppose us."

"Who?"

Highway looks up at the dark sky and then back at me. "Between you and me and not to go any further?"

"Yes," I reply without hesitation.

"Has to be the Diablos. They're the only ones big enough to strike at us. We have a long history with them, but lately, it's been strained. They could be using the Wheelers to push us out."

Surprised at his confession, I say, "I didn't think you'd tell me."

"A wise man said if I trust you, I need to let you in, but make it clear you can't discuss it with anyone."

"I won't."

Highway smiles down at me. "I know."

The Royal Bastards are a unit, stronger together. And somehow, I've breached their walls, and I'm in the inner circle.

All of us go back to where we left the bikes.

Highway gets on his Harley and holds his hand out to me. With a quick motion, I climb on and wrap my arms around his waist.

"Where to?"

Highway places a hand over my own. "Back to the clubhouse. We show Creed your photos and plan our next move."

***

My heart hammers in my chest as I walk into the dimly lit clubhouse, the heavy door slamming shut behind me. The others are already here—Winchester, Justice, Creed, and Reaper—all fierce eyes and clenched jaws.

"What was in the crates that the Crimson Wheelers took?" I ask.

Creed grins. "Powdered sugar, mostly." His arm is in a sling, and he winces as he shifts in his seat. "You've got pictures?"

"Yeah."

"Good." His gaze lands on Winchester. "Anything else?"

"We've got a rat."

Creed cocks his head to the side, his features a mask of anger. "One of us?"

Winchester shakes his head. "I don't think so, but someone we trust."

"For fuck's sake, Winchester, who do you think?" demands Creed.

"It has to be someone who goes unnoticed, but we feel comfortable talking in front of them."

All eyes come to me.

I hold up my hands. "Not me. I would never betray the club."

"Not you, but a female?" Creed's gaze sharpens as he redirects his attention back to Winchester.

"Yeah, it's what I'm thinking or a prospect, but that's unlikely." Winchester screws up his face in a scowl. "Or a brother's family member who overheard them talk about the rally and the delivery."

The men go quiet, each lost in their thoughts.

Highway points at me. "You could find out."

"Me? How?"

"You're new, and if Winchester is right, you'd be in a better position to find out who helped them. Make friends with the women, find out their secrets." Highway looks at Creed, who nods. "I can feel out the prospects, and maybe Reaper and Winchester might see if there's anyone linked to our members who's disgruntled."

Creed chuckles and looks at me. "You keep sticking your nose in where it's not wanted. We could let the club know you're housebound until we decide what to do with you. This could make the rat befriend you."

"Creed, how many women are around the club?" I ask.

"A lot. We don't talk business in front of them, but..." he points at Reaper before he says, "... if someone is having his dick sucked, he might let something slip."

Reaper stands. "The only person sucking my dick is Lucy, and she wouldn't tell anyone anything." Spittle flies from his lips, and his eyes blaze with anger.

"Calm down, Reap."

"You're making accusations about *my* woman. How would you feel if I implied it was Devil?"

Creed's lips turn down, and he tilts his head. "You have a point."

Winchester interjects, "It's not going to be an Ol' Lady."

"How do you know?" Creed asks.

"I don't for sure, but unless someone..." he smirks at Reaper, "... is letting someone other than their Ol' Lady suck their dick, they're loyal. Gotta be a club whore or a hanger-on. It's where Gwen should start."

Reaper smiles. "Can't call her Gwen. She needs a name." He quirks an eyebrow at Highway. "Lyric?"

"What? No. What's wrong with Gwen?" I ask.

"I like it. Lyric is all about the words," says Highway.

"How does that make sense?" The men all ignore

me as they nod in agreement with Reaper. "Gwen is shorter. I like being called Gwen."

Creed stands. "Lyric, welcome to the clubhouse. Be careful, and from here on out, you belong to Highway."

"Wait!" Justice stands. "Why him?"

Creed smirks. "If you have to ask, you haven't been paying attention." He points at Highway. "Keep her safe. I need rest. Painkillers are wearing off, and this hurts like a bitch."

"Hold on a minute. Do I get a say in all of this?"

The men exchange a glance before Creed says, "You could have gotten yourself killed by following the Khans. *We* saved your life, and because you are so eager to help, we're going to let you."

"No, it's not that. I don't mind helping, but why do I belong to Highway?"

Reaper laughs. "Maybe it's not just Justice who hasn't been paying attention." He quirks an eyebrow at Highway. "You got this?"

He nods. "Yeah, I've got this."

Chapter 9

HIGHWAY

As the others leave, either retreating to their rooms or vanishing into the night, Gwen remains lingering with me in the club's dim light. Extending my hand toward her, I silently invite her, and after a hesitant pause, she intertwines her fingers with mine. We ascend the stairs, our footsteps echoing softly against the wooden treads until we reach my room.

"What are we doing?" she queries, her voice tinged with uncertainty.

I kick off my boots with a thud, then loosen my belt, letting my jeans slide down my legs before discarding my T-shirt. Gwen turns away, her gaze fixed firmly on the door.

"Feeling bashful all of a sudden?" I tease gently.

"Just because your friends have some archaic notion of ownership over women doesn't mean I'm obligated to adhere to it," she retorts, her words edged with defiance.

"Gwen—" I start, only to be interrupted by her cutting remark.

"Don't you mean Lyric?" Her new nickname drips with disdain.

"I haven't slept much, and I'm guessing you haven't either. All I want is to hold you and drift off to sleep," I confess earnestly.

She pivots back to face me. "Is that all?"

I can't help but chuckle at her unexpected response. "Now you sound disappointed."

A blush creeps up her neck, and she shakes her head. "N-no."

Cupping her face, I kiss her lips and rest my forehead on hers. "Sleep, for now."

"Okay," she whispers.

Pulling back the covers, I get into bed. Gwen follows suit, shedding her boots and jeans before settling beside me. She rests her head gently on my chest, and when I wrap my arm securely around her waist, a sense of completeness washes over me.

With her warm body against mine and the rhythmic rise and fall of her breathing, it feels like coming home. At this moment, with her nestled close to me, there's an undeniable sense of belonging. It's as if the universe has aligned, and everything falls into place perfectly. And as I close my eyes, I savor the moment, grateful for the woman in my bed.

***

Pounding on my door wakes me, and Gwen sits bolt upright.

"What?" I yell through the door.

"You going to sleep all day?" yells Justice.

"Fuck off," I mumble as I crawl out of bed and open the door. "What time is it?"

He looks past me to Gwen and frowns. "It's ten and..." he pokes me in the chest, "... you're wanted downstairs."

Closing the door, I put my back to it and stare at Gwen. "You okay?"

"Yeah."

"You know, I had plans for you today."

Gwen puts her feet on the floor and bends to pick up her jeans. "What type of plans?"

"The kind that has you begging for more but not getting what you want."

Gwen freezes and looks up at me. "What do you mean?"

"You disobeyed me, and I was going to teach you a lesson."

Gwen puts her feet into her jeans and stands, dragging them up her legs. "Technically, I didn't disobey you."

"But you knew following me was wrong."

Gwen tilts her head from side to side. "Yes and no. You didn't share with me, so I thought I'd find out for myself. I was trying to help."

Pushing off the door, I sit on the bed near her and run a hand from the top of her back to her knee.

"Hmm..."

Gwen turns and kneels in front of me. "I'm sorry."

My cock goes hard, and I'm naked so she can see. "Prove it."

Gwen glances at the door. "Do we have time?"

Grimacing, I say, "No."

Her hand grips my cock, and she moves it up and down. "I can be quick."

With reluctance, I stop her. "Being quick with you is the last thing I want."

Gwen sits back on her heels. "Later?"

I nod, and she stands.

"You can count it." My hand snakes out, and I grab her wrist. "Remember who you belong to."

Gwen laughs. "We will see... on both counts."

As she challenges me, I'm struck by the realization of just how much I want her and how much she belongs with me. But I can't let that desire overwhelm me or scare her away. So, consciously tempering my intensity, I tighten my grip on her wrist just a fraction, my voice softening. "No. In this clubhouse, you belong to me. No more flirting with

Justice. No more flirting with anyone. You want to sell being Lyric, then you act like you belong to me."

"But it's just make-believe, right?"

I swallow hard, feeling the weight of her gaze. This woman tests me in ways I never expected. And though every fiber of my being wants to claim her completely, I know I must tread carefully and show her that belonging to me doesn't mean losing herself in the process.

"For now." I wink at her and stand. "Now, go. You've got work to do." Gwen tries to pull her wrist out of my grasp, but I hold on. "And if you see Justice, tell him I'll be down in a minute."

Then I lean into her and press my lips to hers, a gentle caress at first. The world around us fades away, lost in the sensation of her lips moving against mine, soft and yielding beneath the pressure of my kiss. I drink her in, savoring the taste of her and the sweetness of her breath mingling with mine in a symphony of desire.

And at this moment, as our lips move in a dance of passion, I know with absolute certainty this is where I belong, lost in the intoxicating embrace of her kiss.

Abruptly, I end it before it goes any further and rest my forehead on hers. "Think of that while you're away from me."

Her breaths are ragged, and my heart beats a little faster as she smiles at me. "See you later."

I let her go, and she slips out the door, closing it behind her. With a soft exhale, I shake off the remnants of our encounter, the weight of her absence already settling in the empty space she leaves behind.

Turning away, I rifle through my drawers for clean clothes and then walk to the shower.

***

The MC has been my life for more years than I care to count. One of my favorite things to do is to work behind the bar and serve my brothers. Some think this is beneath me as I'm road captain and should pass it on to one of the prospects. But something they don't realize is everyone talks to me. They share all their secrets, and if I can help, even without their knowledge, I do. Which makes me think it isn't a prospect who betrayed us. They are all so eager to please and to be in our brotherhood. It could be one of our patched-in brothers' family member, but they all know the score. Creed has mellowed since Devil came into his life, but he's still the toughest motherfucker I know. It doesn't sit right with me that it would be someone so close to us. Thinking about it, it troubles me we have a rat.

Today, the air feels charged with something different. The other two chapters are departing on Creed's orders. He's determined to prevent any further harm or tragedy under his watch. I stand behind the bar, methodically polishing glasses, when Missy, one of the club's whores, sidles up beside me.

"What's the deal?" she asks, her curiosity palpable.

"Dutch and Una are heading back home."

"To the UK?"

I put down the glass I'm cleaning and pick up another one. "Yeah. He wants his woman safe, and I don't blame him. And Ghost from our Iowa chapter is headed back today as well."

Missy smiles and nudges me. "He's one tall glass of water I could drink all day."

"Pretty sure he's got a woman."

"So? What happens on a ride stays on a ride. Besides, he might like me better."

Shaking my head, I say, "Don't you want to be more than a fuck? Try saying no, and maybe one of the guys will want you as his permanent ride, but if you give it willingly to everyone and anyone who smiles at you, you'll only ever be a club whore."

Missy sizes me up, a smirk playing on her lips. "Ran into your woman in the kitchen this morning," she remarks casually. "Never pegged you for a one-woman man."

"Who says I am?" I counter, grabbing another glass.

She scoffs. "*She* did."

"Lyric is different, but give her a chance. Show her around, will you?"

Missy picks up a glass and pours herself a whiskey. "Why should I? And who gave *Lyric* her club name?"

"Don't be a bitch, Missy. I want her to like it here, and Reaper called her Lyric."

"Why?" Missy presses, her curiosity piqued.

"Why do I want her to feel welcome, or why did Reaper call her Lyric?" She throws back the whiskey, grits her teeth, and looks me in the eyes. "Both."

"Maybe I want to be a one-woman man, and she's a journalist, so Reaper thought Lyric summed her up," I assert, holding my ground.

"You're letting an outsider, a damn journalist, into our clubhouse? And you even gave her a nickname?" Missy's incredulous tone cuts through the air.

Setting the rag aside, I meet her gaze squarely. "What's your issue?"

Her voice takes on a hint of petulance. "Why haven't I been given a nickname?"

Feral, lounging at the bar, interjects with a teasing grin, "Because you're nothing but a bicycle that everyone's ridden."

Missy slams her glass down, the sound reverberating through the room, and storms off into the kitchen.

"What the hell, Feral?" I reprimand, disbelief coloring my tone.

He shrugs, a picture of innocence. "What?"

I confront him, exasperated. "Why would you say that?"

His eyes roll skyward. "It's the truth."

Justice, seated nearby, chimes in solemnly, "Yes, it's true, but Missy has been with us for five years. She deserves some respect."

Feral's laughter fills the room, but I shake my head in disappointment. "Justice is right. Missy might not be a Bastard, but she's stood by us through thick and thin."

Feral waves a hand in the air. "I'll go apologize."

He slides off the barstool and goes into the kitchen.

"You think he's really going to apologize to her?" asks Justice.

I shrug. "If we hear screaming, we'll know he fucked it up."

Creed steps up to the bar. "Water."

There's more color to his complexion, but from the set of his mouth, I'd say he's still in a world of pain. I pour him a glass, he puts pills in his mouth and washes them down.

"Thanks."

"Any time, Prez." I stare at his shoulder. "How's it feeling?"

"Hurts like a bitch. But I'll heal." He winces as he

leans against the bar. "Where's Lyric?"

"Not sure."

He quirks an eyebrow at me. "Well, you best find out."

Justice smirks at Creed's reprimand, and I scowl at him. "How about you man the bar while I go find *my* woman?"

The smirk falls off his face as I walk into the kitchen, where I find Feral balls deep inside Missy.

"Jesus, Feral! We cook food in here." Shaking my head, I continue through the kitchen and out the backdoor, where I see a group of women.

Lyric is sitting between Devil and Lucy. Opposite them is Nerd, who is the Ol' Lady of Fingers, our computer hacker, and four club whores. They're laughing, having a great time. It's nice to see Lyric smile. She catches me watching, and her smile gets bigger. Lyric gives me a small wave, and the other women all turn to see who she's waving at. Lucy says something, and they all laugh loudly.

"What's so funny?" I ask as I approach them.

"My sister has a permanent smile on her face. I'm guessing it's something you did, Highway." Lucy nudges Lyric, who shakes her head.

"Ignore them. They're all jealous," replies Lyric, and the women laugh loudly.

Devil stands. "I should be getting back to Creed."

"He's in the bar. He looks better."

Devil nods. "He should be resting, but you know

how he is." She reaches down and touches Lyric's shoulder. "See you later?"

Lyric smiles up at her. "Yeah, I'll be around."

Devil winks down at her and heads toward the backdoor.

"Wait!" I yell. "Go around the front."

"Why?"

"Trust me, you do not want to see what's happening in there. Feral is... *busy*."

"Eww, in the kitchen? Who with?" Devil holds up a hand. "No, never mind. I don't want to know." She makes a detour and heads for the front of the clubhouse. "Highway, make sure to tell him to use disinfectant on any surface he may have touched with *any* part of his body."

Chuckling, I say, "Will do." Looking down at Lyric, she's staring up at me with a huge grin. "Take a walk with me?"

"Is that code for let's have sex?" asks Lucy.

The women all laugh. I ignore them and hold out a hand to Lyric. She nods and puts her hand in mine.

"You're all just jealous," Lyric says as she stands.

"Keep telling yourself that," teases Nerd.

"Ladies," I say by way of a goodbye and give them a two-fingered wave. Pulling Lyric along, I entwine my fingers with hers. "Did you learn anything?"

"Too early to tell. Did you want something?"

"No. Creed asked me if I knew where you were."

Rubbing my chin, I continue, "Actually, it felt more like an order."

"Ahh, making sure everyone knows who I belong to."

"Maybe." I glance back at the women. "Who are the others? I know Nerd, she's Fingers' Ol' Lady, but the others not so much."

"Really? They've been with the club for over a year. I thought, as the bartender, you'd know everyone."

"I know them, but I don't *know* them. The one with the black and purple hair helps out in the kitchen now and again. Think her name is Sarah."

"Suzie," Lyric corrects. "She likes it here. Spends most of her nights in Bullet's room."

Bullet is a soldier in our chapter.

"Hell, I didn't even know he was seeing anyone on the regular."

Lyric laughs. "I didn't say that." She looks back at the women. "But she is hoping to be his permanent ride."

"Permanent ride?" I bark out a laugh. "He doesn't seem the type."

"That's what the redhead, Raven said. She has her eye on one of the prospects. I think she said his name was Shadow."

"Sounds like you've all been swapping war stories."

Lyric pulls on my hand. "I didn't swap anything.

You're too important. I'm trying really hard not to fuck this up."

Bending, I steal a kiss. "Do as you're told, and you'll be fine."

Lyric frowns. "You're still mad?"

"Nope, not mad. Just reminding you, I have a certain way of doing things and don't like to be disobeyed."

"Bossy."

Smirking, I kiss her again. "You have no idea." We walk into the clubhouse. "I better get back to work."

Lyric nods at Feral, who's sitting at the bar. "I thought he was busy?"

"Feral isn't known for being gentle. He takes what he wants from those who will let him." In a quieter voice, I say, "Just don't be alone with him in a room, okay?"

Lyric's eyes go wide, and she nods. "Should I check on whoever he was with?"

"She looked fine, but yeah. It was Missy in the kitchen."

Lyric goes up on her tiptoes, kisses me hard, leans back, and smiles at me. "See you later."

She sways her hips and saunters into the kitchen. Feral's eyes are glued to her ass as she passes by. Something akin to anger pulses through me, and as I approach Feral and see his salacious smile, it boils over, and I kick his stool, sending him sprawling to the floor.

"What the fuck?" Feral roars and scrambles to his feet. His arms are outstretched, and he glares at me.

"Keep your fucking eyes off my woman."

"Highway," says Justice. "Calm down. It's Feral. It's what he does."

"Not to her. Not now, not ever."

Feral's nostrils are flared, and he's breathing deeply. He drops his arms, fists clenched as though he's going to hit me.

"Feral, walk it off," orders Creed.

Feral quickly shakes his head, his eyes never leaving me.

"Feral, walk it off so I can talk with Highway."

Nodding profusely, a smirk goes across Feral's face. "Yeah, okay... sure, Prez. You talk to Highway." He walks past me, and his shoulder rams into me. "I'll be outside if you want to talk to me later, Highway."

I take two steps to grab him, but I'm stopped by Creed, who stands between us.

"Let him go."

"The little fucker—"

"I don't care. Let. It. Go."

There's a tense silence as Feral saunters out, leaving me seething. Creed turns his attention to me, his eyes hard and unwavering.

"You need to control your temper, Highway. This isn't the time or place for this."

"He disrespected her," I snap, my fists clenched, knuckles white.

"And you think fighting him is going to solve anything? We've got bigger problems than Feral's wandering eyes."

I take a deep breath, trying to steady myself. The room feels like it's closing in, the tension thick enough to cut with a knife. Creed is right, but the anger still simmers beneath the surface.

"I can't just stand by and let him look at her like that," I mutter, more to myself than to Creed.

"I get it," Creed says, his tone softening slightly. "But you need to pick your battles. This isn't one of them. Have you seen how he stares at Devil or any of the other ol' ladies? Let it go. Feral simply wants what we have. A woman of his own."

I nod reluctantly, the rage slowly ebbing away. Feral is outside, and part of me wants to follow him to settle this once and for all. But Creed's words echo in my mind, reminding me of the bigger picture.

Justice steps closer, placing a hand on my shoulder. "Come on, let's get a drink and cool off. We've got more important things to focus on."

I follow him to the bar, my mind still racing but my body slowly relaxing. Feral's laugh echoes from outside, but I force myself to ignore it—for now.

Chapter 10

Lyric

Missy stands at the sink, her back to me, shoulders moving up and down as though she's crying. The soft, muffled sound of her sobs tug at me. I clear my throat, and her hands fly to her face as she wipes away her tears.

"Are you okay?"

Turning around, Missy forces a smile. "I'm just peachy. How are you, Lyric?" Her eyes are red and puffy, the remnants of her tears still visible.

"You don't seem fine." I point over my shoulder. "I just saw Feral at the bar. Did he—"

Missy's hands fly in the air, her face contorting with rage. "That little motherfucker! I bet he couldn't wait to tell everyone, could he? Yeah, so what? I fucked him. He lasted all of a minute with his micropenis!"

Surprised at her outburst, I hold up my hands. "No, you misunderstand me. I thought he might have hurt you. I came in here to check on you, to make sure you're okay."

Missy strides toward me, eyes blazing, shaking her head. "Sure you did. Little Miss 'I've been here all of a week and now have Highway all to myself.' How long do you think that will last before he's sticking his dick somewhere else? You don't think I haven't had that man inside me?" She smiles and nods slowly, a triumphant glint in her eye. "I've let him fuck me any way he wants." Missy puts her hands on her hips and licks her lips. "He'll be back. They always come back."

"Yeah, but they don't stay."

Missy looks taken aback. "What?"

Crossing my arms across my chest, I give her a once-over. "I came in here to be a friend to you, Missy. I was concerned about you. Do you have any female friends? I'm thinking no. You see, Missy, good women lift each other up and aren't in competition with them. But you?" I shake my head. "Do you really think you have a chance with any of the men in the MC? You don't because they can tell you're damaged goods, and no one wants to keep damaged goods. Sure, you might be used from time to time, but not forever."

Missy lets out an almighty scream, reverberating through the kitchen. She lunges at me, her eyes wild with fury. Her nails slash through the air, narrowly missing my face as I sidestep, but I feel a sharp sting as they scrape down my arm. Pain flares, but I don't hesitate. Drawing back my fist, I channel all my anger and frustration into a single punch. It connects with the side of her jaw, a solid impact that sends her spinning. She crashes into the kitchen counter, a mix of shock and pain flashing across her face as she slams against it.

"You fucking bitch!" Missy screams.

"Calm the fuck down." I have my hands in front of me as I back away from her.

"You think you're better than me? You're not. None of you are. You're all club whores." Missy's voice is sharp and bitter as she picks up a knife from the kitchen counter, her knuckles white from gripping it so tightly.

"Missy, you don't want to do this." My voice trembles slightly, but I hold my ground.

A tear rolls down her cheek as she hesitantly steps toward me. "Maybe I do. I'm so sick of being the club's plaything. I want to be an Ol' Lady, but women like you keep showing up and stealing what's mine."

"Highway was never yours." My words hang in the air, charged with tension.

The kitchen door bursts open, and Highway strides in. His eyes dart from me to Missy and back, surprise momentarily crossing his face before a more primal and dangerous look takes over. In a flash, he rushes past me and grabs Missy's wrist, the one with the knife. "Drop it, or I'll drop you," he growls out, his voice low and menacing.

"She started it," Missy whines, her voice trembling.

"And I'm ending it," Highway states firmly.

The knife slips from Missy's grasp, clattering loudly on the kitchen floor. Highway's intense gaze shifts to me, his expression softening slightly.

"Are you okay?" he asks, concern evident in his eyes.

The scratch marks down my arm sting, and I notice a trickle of blood dripping onto the floor. "I'm fine," I reply, trying to sound more confident than I feel.

Highway's eyes narrow as he looks at my arm. "You don't look fine. Go see Justice… get him to take you to medical. I'll be along in a minute."

I nod, reluctantly turning to leave.

The adrenaline still courses through my veins, and my heart pounds as I make my way out of the kitchen, leaving Highway to deal with Missy.

Chapter 11

Highway

Tears stream down Missy's face as she backs away from me, shaking uncontrollably. She wraps her arms around herself, trying to hold it together.

"What the fuck happened?" I ask, my voice steely with confusion and concern.

"Does it matter? You're going to be on *her side*!" she screams, her voice raw with pain. "*Lyric...*" she spits out the name as if it's poison. "She's been here all of a hot minute, and she's one of us?" She points to herself, her hand trembling. "I've cooked, cleaned, and fucked most of you, but I'm still Missy. I'm still overlooked and treated like garbage."

I shake my head, feeling a pang of guilt. "I sent Lyric in here to check up on you and make sure you're okay. You're not overlooked, Missy."

Her voice drops to a whisper, her eyes fixed on

the floor. "But I'm not one of you either."

She looks defeated, her spirit crushed, and although I don't like seeing her like this, she had a knife in her hand when I walked in. I step closer, but she flinches, so I stop.

"Missy, please look at me," I whisper. "You're important to us."

She lifts her eyes, filled with tears and hurt. "You say that, but it doesn't feel true. When Lyric showed up, everything changed. She fits in so easily like she was meant to be here."

I reach out, hesitating, before gently placing my hand on her shoulder. "Lyric's presence doesn't change your value. You've been with us for years."

Her lips tremble as she tries to hold back more tears. "Then why do I feel so alone?"

My chest tightens. "I regret if we've made you feel that way."

She takes a shaky breath, her eyes searching mine for any sign of deceit. "Do you really mean that?"

I nod, squeezing her shoulder gently. "Yes, I do. We'll make this right. I'll make this right."

For a moment, we stand in silence, the weight of our words hanging in the air. Slowly, she relaxes, her grip on herself loosening.

"Okay," Missy whispers, her voice fragile but tinged with hope. She nods, a small, tentative smile forming on her lips. "I wouldn't have hurt her."

She twists toward me, attempting to kiss me. I place both hands firmly on her shoulders and push her back. Despite her hard work and dedication to the club, I've never been intimate with her, and I don't intend to start. Missy *is* a club whore and not someone I want to get involved with.

"What?" she asks, confusion flashing across her face.

"I'm with Lyric."

"But you haven't made her your Ol' Lady. I won't tell."

I step back, putting some distance between us. "I like you, Missy, but I'm not interested in you that way."

Her face flushes red with anger, and she throws her hands in the air. "You're just like all the others!"

The door to the kitchen swings open, and Creed walks in. "What the fuck is going on?" he demands.

Shaking my head, I point at Missy. "I'm not entirely sure."

Creed looks her up and down, a stern expression on his face. "What did I tell you?"

"To keep my crazy under control," she mutters.

Surprised at her words, I cock my head to the side and look at Creed. "She done this before?"

Creed's eyebrows knit together. "What did she do?"

"Nothing!" Missy cries.

Creed ignores her, staring directly at me. "What?"

"I walked in. She had a knife in her hands and was going after Lyric."

Creed's head snaps back in Missy's direction. "You were warned."

"I didn't touch her!"

"Not true. Lyric had scratch marks down her arm. You did that."

Missy closes the gap between us and clutches my shirt desperately. "You said you'd help me." Tears and sobs escape her, her eyes searching mine for a shred of compassion.

"You're done."

Creed's words cause Missy to freeze. Her eyes glaze over, and she stops crying. I gently pry her hands off me and step back, but Missy doesn't seem to notice. Her hands remain bunched together as if I'm still standing there.

"Did you hear me?" Creed asks, his tone firm.

"N-no." Missy's hands drop to her sides, her voice barely a whisper. "We're family."

"Last time I checked, a family doesn't go after each other with knives." Creed casts a glance at me. "Escort her out."

I nod and move toward Missy, who seems lost in her own world. "Come on, Missy," I say softly, trying to guide her toward the door.

Her eyes flicker with a mixture of confusion and

despair. "But... where will I go?"

"You'll figure it out," I reply, my voice gentle but firm. "But you can't stay here."

She takes a hesitant step, then another, her shoulders slumped in defeat. As we reach the door, she pauses and looks back at Creed, a silent plea in her eyes.

Creed's expression remains stern. "This is for the best, Missy. You were warned, and I've had enough of your temper."

Missy pushes me away and screams at Creed, "You think you're in a world of pain now?" Hysterical laughter spills out of her. "Just you wait and see!"

Missy runs away from us, and I look at Creed. "Do I follow?"

"No, let her go. She's been on the edge of psycho town for a while. Lyric isn't the first woman Missy's tried to carve up, but she will be the last."

Creed walks back into the front of the clubhouse, and I follow him. There are at least a dozen brothers waiting near the bar.

Creed holds a hand in the air. "Missy is banned from the compound. Make sure everyone knows. I don't care if you seek her out, but she's not to ride on our bikes and not allowed to our rallies or parties. Missy is dead to us."

"Why?" asks Feral.

Creed gives him a scathing look. "Because I said

so. No one goes after one of our women without consequences. Hell, she's lucky I didn't shoot her."

Feral looks down at his feet, nods, and walks out of the clubhouse.

I lock eyes with Reaper, who takes a deep breath and follows Feral.

"Go check on Lyric," Creed orders.

"She sliced Lyric?" asks Ghost, his blue eyes going frosty.

I stop and look at him. "No, man. I stopped that, but she scratched her up pretty good."

"Gotta say Missy was one persistent woman. They can poison a club."

I dip my chin and keep moving. Before I enter the room where Lyric is, I see Ghost and Dutch deep in a hushed conversation with Creed.

"Hey, you," says Lyric as soon as I enter.

Justice is dabbing her scratches with what smells like antiseptic.

"How's the arm?"

Lyric winces as Justice touches her again. I hold out my hand, and he hands over the gauze.

"It's fine."

"I better get back to the bar." Justice nods at me and heads for the door.

"Thank you," Lyric calls out as he disappears.

"You know, if these look red or swollen, you might need a tetanus shot," I say as I gently inspect her arm.

"I had one two years ago when I was in Afghanistan."

"What set Missy off?"

Lyric shrugs. "I have no idea."

I put my arms around her and kiss the top of her head. "I'm glad you're okay."

Her arms wrap around my waist. "I'm glad you walked in when you did. Where is Missy?"

"Creed banished her."

Lyric leans back to look into my eyes. "Over me?"

"No. You were the final straw. She's been erratic for a while." I cup her face with my hands. "Are you okay?"

"Do you think it could be Missy who ratted you out to Crimson Wheelers?"

Shaking my head, I say, "No way."

"Why? Because she was one of your... special friends?"

My hands drop from her face, and I burst out laughing. "Special friends?"

Lyric steps away from me. "Yes, or would you prefer I said fuck buddy?"

Trying not to laugh, I say, "I never fucked Missy."

Lyric nods, and her eyes drop to my chest. "Oh."

"Yeah, oh."

"But she said..."

Putting two fingers under her chin, I tilt her head back. "Yeah, some of the club girls gossip, and I'm not saying I haven't ever had sex with anyone but you." Her eyes come back to mine. "But I am saying I'd like it to be *just you* for the foreseeable future."

"Just me?"

"Yeah. How about we see how this thing goes?"

Lyric swallows and then, in a quiet voice, says, "I'd like that."

My hand drops to my side. "Come here."

She closes the gap between us and squeezes me tight. "Wanna go upstairs and fool around?"

Creed clears his throat behind us. "Highway, you got a minute?"

I kiss her forehead and turn. "Yeah, Prez."

"Meeting room, now."

Lyric puts her hand in mine. "That sounds serious."

"I'll tell you later."

"Really?"

"Yeah, you're in this now. But what is said between us stays between us."

Lyric smiles, and I kiss her once more before entering the meeting room.

Stepping into the room, I'm surprised to see Dutch and Ghost sitting at our table. Their expressions are serious, and my heart beats a little faster.

Creed wastes no time with pleasantries. "Highway, we suspect Missy has been feeding information to the Crimson Wheelers."

For a moment, I'm stunned as disbelief washes

over me. But as the accusation sinks in, surprise quickly turns to anger.

"What the hell? Missy? Are you sure?" My fists clench at my sides. "What's our next move?"

Chapter 12

Lyric

It's been a hell of a few days, and I'm beat. Reaching into my pocket, I still have Winchester's truck keys. I walk back into the clubhouse and see him sitting at a table, eyes fixed on the meeting room's closed door.

"Hey." I jiggle the keys in his face. "Do you mind if I borrow your truck?"

His eyes flick to me, then back to the door. "I thought you were housebound?"

"I need to get some personal items from home. I'll be an hour tops."

Winchester squints at me. "Only an hour?"

"Yep."

"Okay."

"Thanks. If Highway is looking for me, I'll be at home."

"I'll let him know."

Outside, Justice is talking to another MC member and pauses to smile at me as I walk past. I keep going until I get to Winchester's truck, and as I open the door, Justice taps me on the shoulder.

"I guess I'm no longer taking you to the swamp?"

I climb into the truck. "No. I don't think Highway would approve."

He rubs his chin thoughtfully. "Highway, huh? Never would have pegged you as liking him."

Not knowing what to say, I start the truck's engine. "Thanks for looking after my arm."

"My pleasure, and if you get sick of Highway, I'll be around." He grins at me, shuts the truck's door, and walks away.

Gripping the truck's wheel, I pull out onto the highway. The road is clear, and the sun is shining brightly. I'm humming along to the radio when I see a woman walking alongside the road.

Missy.

There's no mistaking her defiant walk, the way her boots hit the pavement with purpose, even though she's got nowhere to call home. My gut twists. I shouldn't stop, the club has rules about trust and loyalty, but dammit, something pulls me over.

"Need a lift?" My voice cuts through the quiet like a knife.

She hesitates, her eyes narrowing, searching for

the catch. But desperation wins, and she climbs into the passenger seat, the door slamming shut with finality. "Thanks," she mutters, words barely more than a breath.

"How far are you headed?"

"Far enough." Her gaze stays glued to the window, watching the world blur by.

"Nice day, huh?" The words feel stupid as they tumble out, but I can't help it. I need to fill the space with something other than tension.

"Sure." She doesn't look at me or bite on the small-talk bait.

The silence stretches between us. I focus on the road, the lines flashing by one after another, marking distance and time. Before long, I break the silence again. "Something on your mind?" I venture again, pushing.

"Nothing worth talking about."

"Not even an apology for attacking me?"

Slowly, Missy turns her head to look at me. "You look fine." She takes a deep breath. "And I wouldn't have stabbed you."

"Still hurts like a bitch."

"Why'd you pick me up?"

"It's not safe for a woman to be walking along the highway alone."

Missy scowls at me. "So they didn't send you?"

"Why would they send me?"

Missy's silence gnaws at me, loud and sharp.

My ringtone slices through the cab. My heart jolts. The screen lights up—Highway. I snatch the phone from the cup holder.

"Talk to me," I answer, my thumb pressed hard against the wheel.

"Lyric—" His voice is that low rumble I know too well, but before he can lay another word on me she interrupts.

"Are you serious?" Missy's outburst shatters the quiet, her voice like shrapnel. "You and Highway? What does he even see in you?"

I blink, stunned, fumbling with the phone. It nearly slips from my grasp.

"Missy, what are you—"

"He's been single for years, and suddenly you swoop in, and poof, you're part of the family?" She spits the words, venom and envy tangling together. "How did you manage to get a club name before me? You don't belong here, Lyric."

"Hey!" I snap back, heat coursing through my veins, tension coiling tight in my chest. "That's enough!"

My grip on the steering wheel is white-knuckled, my breaths coming fast. "Highway, I'll call you back," I say into the phone and end the call without waiting for an answer.

Missy's chest heaves, her anger a live wire between us.

"Missy..." I start, voice steel-hard, "... we're

109

gonna settle this. But not on the road."

My heart hammers in my chest, a drumbeat loud enough to drown out the engine's roar. Missy's fists are clenched like she's ready for a fight.

"Tell me one thing, Lyric," she says, voice low and dangerous. "Why do you and your sister get everything? What's so special about you two?"

"Missy, I—" Again, she cuts me off.

"Shut it! You think you're part of them now?" A bitter laugh escapes her. "You have no idea what goes on. No idea what I've done."

The road before us gives way to the chaos of downtown Jacksonville. My fists are clenched tightly on the wheel, every muscle tensed, waiting for whatever comes next.

"You want to know something, Lyric?" She leans closer, and I can feel the heat of her breath. "I was the one who tipped off the Crimson Wheelers. Told 'em where the Royal Bastards would be that day. *Me.*"

Time stops. The words hang heavy between us, thick with treachery. It's like a bomb has been dropped in the cab. My foot slams onto the brakes, the tires screech against the asphalt, and the world turns into a chaotic blur.

"Missy!" My voice cracks like a whip. "How could you betray the club?"

Her face is a mask of defiance, eyes alight with some wild, desperate fire. But beneath it all, I see it—the flicker of fear. She knows she's crossed a line—one she can't uncross.

"Missy," I say again, ice lacing through my tone. The truck idles, a beast growling beneath us, mirroring the storm inside me. "Start talking."

Missy's eyes dart from me to the open road and back again. She reaches for the door handle, hesitation written all over her face for just a split second before she decides. The door swings open, and she bolts, her boots slapping against the pavement as she runs for the mouth of an alleyway.

"Dammit!" I hiss under my breath, but I don't follow. Instead, I watch her disappear into the belly of Jacksonville, swallowed up between the buildings.

I grab my phone. My thumb hovers over it before I punch in the number. It rings. Once. Twice.

"Highway," his voice rumbles through the speaker.

"Missy bolted," I spit out, my words clipped. "She confessed, she told the Crimson Wheelers where to find the MC leaders at the rally."

"Shit." The curse is a low growl on his end of the line. There's a pause, a breath, then, "We know. Are you safe?"

"Yeah," I say, but there's no relief, only the acid burn of betrayal in my veins.

"Lyric, listen…" Highway's voice cuts through the static of my thoughts. "Head home. Lock up and wait for me."

"Highway—" I begin, but he interrupts.

"Can't talk now. I'll explain everything soon." The line clicks dead before I can protest. His words hang in the air, a command that leaves no room for argument.

I throw the phone onto the car seat with more force than necessary, my pulse thrumming with adrenaline. My grip tightens on the steering wheel, my fingers straining as I steer Winchester's truck through the maze of streets.

My mind races with what Missy said, the betrayal stinging like a fresh wound.

"Damn you, Missy," I mutter under my breath as I make the last turn onto my street.

The house looms ahead. I kill the engine, the sudden silence almost deafening. I'm out of the truck and at the front door in seconds, my movements swift and sure. The key turns in the lock with a click that echoes too loudly in the stillness. On the coat rack is my sister's jacket.

"Lucy?" I call out as I step inside.

"In here," comes the reply from the living room.

I find her curled up on the couch, a book forgotten in her lap, as she looks up at me with wide, worried eyes. "What's wrong?"

"Nothing," I lie smoothly, forcing a smile. "Just one of those days."

She doesn't look convinced, but she nods,

accepting the answer for now. "Be careful, Lyric," she says softly, her gaze piercing.

"Always am," I reply with a wink, though the flutter in my chest belies my casual tone.

"Highway called," she adds, and there's a question in her voice that I'm not ready to answer.

"Everything's fine. He'll fill us in soon."

"Okay," she says, but the concern lingers.

I leave her there with her book and unspoken fears and head to my room. The promise of Highway's explanations does little to ease the tension coiled tight in my muscles, but for now, there's nothing to do but wait.

***

A knock sounds on my front door. When I open it, Highway stands there. I can tell by the set of his jaw that what he's got to say isn't going to be pretty. He walks past me and into the living room where Lucy is waiting.

"Lyric, Lucy, sit down." His voice is gravelly, urgent.

We drop onto the couch, and tension knots in my stomach. Lucy fidgets beside me, her leg bouncing like a piston.

Highway doesn't waste time and gets straight to the punch. "It was Missy who betrayed us," he says, looking at Lucy.

"Missy?" Lucy spits out, disbelief sharpening her tone. "She what? How?"

"She gave the Crimson Wheelers everything."

Lucy's face twists red, her fury almost palpable. We've been double-crossed by one of our own.

"What are we going to do with her?" Lucy growls, her voice strained with wrath.

Highway's lips press into a thin line. He looks at us, his silence heavy as a hammer.

"Lucy, Lyric..." he pauses, choosing his words. "We deal with traitors in one way. But right now, we gotta think ahead."

Highway sits then leans forward, elbows on his knees, hands clasped. "She's out," he says, voice razor-sharp. "Banished. But we can't just let her slink away."

"Can't we?" I ask, heat flaring in my chest.

"No." He shakes his head, a predator ready to pounce. "We need her one last time. To feed the Crimson Wheelers bad intel."

"Bad intel?" Lucy echoes, her brow furrowed.

"About a shipment," Highway continues. "Drugs that ain't coming. See if she bites and passes it to them."

I chew on the inside of my cheek, considering. Could work. Might backfire. "Does Missy have anyone in Jacksonville? Family or friends?"

Highway blinks, confusion clouding his face for a second. "Jacksonville?" He shrugs, a mountain shifting. "No clue."

"Great," I mutter. No ties means no leverage. But also, no place for her to run.

"Any other bright ideas?" Lucy asks.

Highway shrugs, and I pace the room, the weight of betrayal sitting like a lead vest on my shoulders. Missy, for all her faults, was one of us. And now? She's a ghost, haunting the edges of our lives with her treachery.

"Dammit," I hiss under my breath, anger and something else—a twisted kind of pity—warring inside me. Years she rode with them, her laughter as loud as any.

Who really knew her?

Not a soul.

"Hey." I lock eyes with Lucy. "What if we find her? Get her to swallow the bait."

Lucy's lips press into a thin line, her nod slow but sure. "I'm in. Got a hunch where she might drown her sorrows."

"Good." My jaw sets. "We do this together."

"I don't like the idea of you in danger, and Reaper wouldn't like it either," Highway says.

Lucy nods and looks him in the eyes. "I know, but she's never going to believe you or one of the boys, but with us, she might think we're dumb enough to let something slip."

He sighs. "You're right, but I don't have to like it. If you're going to do this, it needs to be somewhere public. I don't want either of you hurt."

"Trust me when I tell you I'm not going to take any chances with my little sister."

I smile at her and Highway. After years of being separated, Lucy and I are back to being the close sisters we once were, and now, with the MC, I think I've found the true meaning of family.

Highway nods. "Stick together," he growls out.

"Got it," I reply, feeling the weight of his reluctance like a second skin.

"Let's roll," Lucy says, her voice all business as she stands.

***

The drive to the first bar takes us to the beach. It's one of those touristy places with lots of people and overpriced drinks.

"Do you really think she'll be in here?"

Lucy shrugs. "She used to come here, and the tourists would buy her drinks. Missy is always looking for what she can get for free or for a quick fuck." Lucy's lips turn down. "Can you imagine fucking someone for a drink?"

We hit the pavement, our boots clicking in unison. The sun dips low, bleeding orange across a bruising sky. Entering the bar, Lucy does a quick scout around and comes back to me.

"She's not here. Let's try the next place."

Bar after bar, we search—eyes sharp, backs straight. Each place is another dead end, another shot of something strong to keep the edge honed.

"Nothing," Lucy mutters, her frustration a live wire.

"Next," I say, the word tasting of dust and determination.

The world dims, streetlights flickering to life as we push on. Finally, we spot her. She's sitting in the back of the bar, alone, with a beer in front of her.

"Found her," I whisper, victory and venom swirling in my chest.

"Time to work," Lucy replies, her eyes narrowing to slits.

Missy doesn't look up or move. She just sits there, a statue carved from regret and cheap whiskey. Missy's gaze doesn't shift or waver—just meets ours and stays, heavy with something that looks a lot like surrender. No fight left in her, no fire. Just defeat, hanging on her like a shroud.

"Missy," Lucy's voice slices through the smoky air, sharp as a blade. "How could you do it? Betray the MC?"

The words hang there between us, thick with accusation. I can almost see them, black against the haze, waiting for an answer. We both pull out chairs and sit opposite her.

She shrugs—a small, tired lift of her shoulders—and there's this hollow look in her eyes as if she's been emptied from within. "Crimson Wheelers said they'd think about making me an Ol' Lady," she confesses, her voice flat like she's reading from a script written by someone else.

I can feel the lie she's telling herself, bitter on my tongue. She knows it's crap, and yet she clings to it so desperately.

"Thought I wanted... someone, something, just for me... my own slice of life." Her voice trembles.

Lucy scoffs, disbelief and anger laced tight in her tone. "And for that, you sold us out?"

Missy doesn't answer or need to. It's all there, written in the slump of her body and the way her hands fidget with the frayed edge of a coaster—a story of longing gone wrong, twisted into betrayal.

I watch her. A part of me understands that raw need to be seen and belong. But understanding doesn't mean forgiving. Not in this world. Not for this.

"You here to give me a beating?"

Lucy shakes her head. "No, not that you don't deserve one." Lucy's top lip curls up in disgust. "You were one of us, and as much as I want to blame you, I was worried and wanted to check on you."

Missy's head snaps up, and she stares Lucy in the eyes. "For real?"

"Yeah." Lucy glances at me then back to Missy.

"Also Creed wanted me to give you a message. You're dead to us. Banished. There's no coming back."

Shaking my head at Missy, I tug on Lucy's hand. "We've gotta go. You've checked on her, but we can't be late."

"Go? Now?" Lucy's voice cuts through the tension, sharp and confused. "Why the hell—"

I shoot her a look, eyes wide, trying to channel every ounce of urgency into my gaze. "The thing, Lucy. We've got that thing."

Her brows knit together, a frown etching across her face. "What thing?"

I huff out an impatient breath, feigning annoyance. "The truck stop... the delivery?" My voice rises, a question hanging in the air between us, waiting for her to grab it.

Recognition flashes over her features, a dawning comprehension. She straightens up and nods slightly. "Right. The truck stop."

Our acting skills won't win us any Oscars, but here's hoping Missy doesn't catch on.

"Could you tell Creed I'm sorry?"

Lucy nods. "I will, but it won't do you any good. See you in the next life."

Missy's face creases, her bottom lip trembling. "I just wanted to be an Ol' Lady."

"And now you never will be. Unless you somehow win over the Crimson Wheelers, but I doubt they'd want you." I gesture to Lucy for us to leave.

She stares at Missy for a moment longer. We push back our chairs, the legs scraping against the grimy floor, and stride toward the exit. My heart is hammering, adrenaline pumping through my veins like fire.

Outside, I cast one last glance back.

There she is, Missy, her cell phone clutched in her hand like a lifeline as she punches in numbers with a shaky finger. A thread of hope unfurls within me, a silent prayer that she's doing exactly what we need her to do.

"Think she bought it?" Lucy's voice is low, a whisper meant only for my ears.

"God, I hope so," I mutter, watching Missy bring the phone to her ear. Her lips move, words spilling out into the void, hopefully sealing the fate we've crafted for the Crimson Wheelers.

"Let's bounce before we draw attention." Lucy grabs my arm, tugging me away from the scene, our boots pounding against the asphalt as we escape.

We slide into Winchester's truck, the interior smelling of leather and motor oil, and I slam the door shut hard enough to echo in the quiet street. I snatch up my phone, punch in Highway's number, each tone a drumbeat in the tense silence between Lucy and me.

"Talk to me," Highway growls on the other end,

his voice gravelly mixed with impatience.

"We dropped the bait," I say, clipped and quick. "Missy's making calls, but we can't be sure if she's swallowing it whole or just nibbling."

"We need this to work," Highway says. "What bar is she at?"

"The last one on Mary Street before you hit Riverside Avenue."

"Thanks for doing that. The club owes you."

"We did what we could." I glance at Lucy, her face set in grim determination. "And the club owes me nothing."

"Keep your eyes sharp," is all he says before the line goes dead.

I toss the phone on the dash, my gut knotted tight as barbed wire. We sit there for a moment, then Lucy nods toward the bar. I swing my gaze back to the grimy windowpanes just in time to see shadows moving inside.

"Shit," I breathe out.

Ghost and Dutch, like twin specters, slip through the bar's entrance, their presence screaming danger more than any siren ever could. The air in the cab turns cold, and I know Missy's world is about to come crashing down hard.

"Endgame," Lucy murmurs, and I can't help but agree.

No more secrets for Missy, none at all.

Chapter 13

Highway

Justice is a silent statue beside me as we hide in the shadows of the warehouse. His eyes are fixed on the closed doorway. We wait for the Crimson Wheelers and the hell we will unleash on them.

"Any minute now," Justice murmurs, the words barely a vibration in the cool night air.

A set of headlights pierces the darkness, and the growl of an engine cuts through the silence. The truck approaches. My hand rests on the cold metal of my piece, comfort in its familiar weight.

"Showtime," I mutter under my breath as the truck's brakes squeal.

One of the prospects, a wiry kid with more guts than brains, swings the doors open. His movements are eager and hungry. The truck rolls in, and we all hold our breath.

"Easy," I breathe, eyeing the shadows where my brothers lie in wait. The Royal Bastards are a pack of wolves ready to strike. But we're not alone in our hunt tonight. The tension is a living thing, coiling around us, ratcheting tighter with each passing second.

The rumble hits us first, a vibration through the concrete. Harleys, too many to count, their roar a challenge that splits the night. Headlights flash as the Crimson Wheelers ride into the warehouse.

"Shit," I hiss, my fingers tightening around the grip of my Glock. They roll in, engines snarling, leather and chrome gleaming under the warehouse lights. These bastards are way too cocky.

"Stay down," Justice commands, his voice barely above a whisper.

They dismount like they own the place, boots striking the floor with the arrogance only fools possess. One of them draws out a gun and shoves it in our prospect's face. The driver's door is flung open, and the driver is staring down the barrel of a gun.

"Outta the truck! Now!" one of the Wheelers bellows, a scarred brute with fists like hammers. He steps forward, gun waving wildly in the air, the authority of violence etched into his every scar.

"Keep cool," I murmur, waiting and watching. It's not time yet, but the itch to act is like a fire in my veins.

"Move it!" Scarface barks at the driver, who's shaking so badly he can barely get his feet to function.

Justice's hand twitches, a signal only I can read. Soon, very soon. The Royal Bastards won't bow to these gutter rats.

"Hey, pretty boy!" Scarface sneers at the prospect, shoving the kid hard enough to make him stumble back. "Next time you open those doors, it'll be the last thing you—" He cuts off, laughter dying in his throat as he catches sight of something beyond the truck. Something he didn't expect.

"Too late now," I whisper.

What comes next is the part I live for, the clash, the fight, the dance with death. We're the Royal Bastards, and this is our turf. These Crimson clowns are about to learn what happens when you crash the wrong party.

Justice steps out, lean and lethal, his eyes all fire and fight. "Evening, fellas," he drawls, stepping into the dim light.

The Wheelers freeze, their bravado flickering. It's like they've seen a ghost, only this ghost has a blade glinting in his hand and a grin that doesn't quite reach his eyes.

"Drop 'em," Creed's voice cuts through the tension, sharp as the edge of Justice's knife. No face, just the command echoing off the warehouse walls.

Gunshots explode as the Crimson Wheelers fire

blindly into the shadows. I hold my ground, heart racing, watching as Justice closes in on Scarface. The burly biker's gun trembles and clatters to the concrete as Justice holds his blade to his neck.

"Easy now," Justice murmurs, but there's steel behind the soft words. The blade kissing Scarface's throat draws a thin red line, a vibrant bloom of red against the paleness of his skin. Scarface's eyes bulge, horror-struck, as his brothers crumple one by one in the dark.

"Didn't have to be this way," Justice says, almost gently.

But we all know it did.

We all know there's no room for mercy.

Silence falls, pierced by the ragged breaths of the living.

I step over a still body, boots sticking slightly to the slick warehouse floor. The tang of gunpowder and blood hangs thick in the air, a scent that is all too familiar.

I move alongside Justice, my gaze darting from shadow to shadow. No movement. Just us and the bodies. The night's chaos is settling into an eerie calm. My fingers loosen around the grip of my Glock, the metal warm from use. With a click, it finds its place at my side, nestled in its holster.

Justice's grip on Scarface hasn't eased. The burly man is trying to swallow, his Adam's apple bobbing against the blade. His eyes are wild, flicking between his fallen brothers and the steel at his throat.

"Who was it?" It's Creed's voice, rough like gravel. He emerges, one arm hanging useless in a sling but the other ready and steady. He's a predator despite his injury, dangerous and demanding answers.

Scarface shakes his head, his lips pressed into a thin line. He knows talking will sign his death warrant, but so is staying silent. Fear has got him in a vice, squeezing tight enough for panic to seep through the cracks.

"Spit it out," Creed pushes, stepping closer.

The burly man's eyes dart to him, then to the floor. Silence won't cut it, not tonight. Not with what's at stake.

The tension is a live wire between us, sparking with every second he keeps his mouth shut. We need answers, and we need them yesterday. This war has been a long time coming, and now it's on our doorstep.

"Talk," Creed growls.

Justice's arm tenses, the knife edge kissing skin. A bead of blood trickles down the man's throat.

Scarface gasps, eyes bulging. "This here, it's nothing. A taste."

"Of what?" Creed's words are ice.

"War," the burly biker spits out. "You took tonight, sure. But what's coming..." He chuckles, but more from fear than bravado.

"The Khans?" Creed probes, eyes narrowed.

Laughter erupts from the man's throat, rich and dark with fake amusement. "No. It's closer than that."

A shadow moves forward—Reaper—vengeance radiating off him, his blade glinting.

The man recognizes him. His eyes go wide, he shakes his head, and then blurts out, "Diablo."

"Diablo," Creed echoes the word. "Shit." He's staring at the dirty concrete beneath us, and I can tell it isn't just the floor he's seeing. Disappointment creases his features, deep lines carved by betrayal.

His head tilts, his eyes locking with Reaper's. A silent conversation passes between them, and the nod that follows is all it takes.

Justice is a coiled spring. He moves, a flicker of motion, and Scarface hits the floor hard. For a heartbeat, the guy looks up, thinking maybe, just maybe, he's dodged a bullet.

He's dead wrong.

Reaper steps forward, swift as a shadow, and there's no hesitation in his movement. Steel flashes, biting deep, tearing through lies and flesh alike.

Blood arcs high, a gruesome fountain painting the night red. A choked gurgle rips from Scarface's throat, the sound raw and primal. His body convulses, thrashing in the dirt on the concrete floor like some wounded animal fighting for its last breath.

"Damn," I mutter under my breath, watching Scarface clutch at his throat.

The man's final spasms slow, then still. The silence that follows is thick enough to choke on. The acrid scent of blood and gunpowder stings my nostrils. My heart hammers in my chest. The body at my feet lies too still—the thrashing stopped, and the gurgling silenced. I watch until the man's eyes fix on a point far beyond this world, the light fading from them as death claims another soul.

"Highway."

Creed's voice slices through the aftermath, quiet but carrying the weight of an order. He doesn't need to say more. We've done this dance before—we know the steps by heart.

"Got it," I reply, my tone even.

I look at him and see the hard set of his jaw and the tightness around his eyes. He's our president, our leader, unshakeable and unbreakable. But tonight, I see something else there, a chink in the armor.

"Make sure they're gone. Every last one," he commands, his words leaving no room for error.

"Understood." I acknowledge with a nod, my gaze sweeping the area.

It's a grim job but necessary. We can't leave any

evidence behind or give the cops or our enemies anextThe anything to work with. We move like ghosts, erasing ourselves from the scene.

As I direct the cleanup, my mind races, piecing together the puzzle of tonight's events.

"Creed," I venture once the others are busy at work. "You think the Diablos are behind this?"

His eyes catch mine in the dim light, hard as flint. For a heartbeat, he's silent, considering, then gives a single, curt nod. No words, but it's all the confirmation I need.

"Shit." The curse is out before I can stop it.

Creed stands there, a solitary figure against the darkness, staring into the night as if he could see right into the heart of our troubles.

"Let's finish here," he says after a moment, his voice rough with unspoken thoughts. "We'll talk back at the clubhouse."

"Roger that." I turn back to the task at hand, but my mind is already racing ahead, thinking of what this means for us, for the Royal Bastards.

If the Diablos are moving against us...

Well, that's a storm we might not weather.

But for now, we clean.

We make it like we were never here.

And we brace for what's coming next.

***

Gravel crunches underfoot as I drag the last of the Crimson Wheelers to the pit we've dug out back. Sweat beads on my brow, mixing with the grime and blood spatters—the scent is metallic. My breath comes in sharp pulls.

"Dump him," Reaper hisses from the edge.

I heave the lifeless body into the dark hole, not bothering to look where it lands. There's no ceremony here, just cold necessity. I wipe my hands on my jeans, feeling the coarse fabric scrape against my skin. The air is heavy with unspoken tension.

"Think we're clear?" Justice's voice cuts through the silence, sharp as his knife.

"Yeah," I grunt, knowing full well the mess we're in now isn't just about tonight—it's about what happens when dawn breaks.

"Diablos won't take this lying down," Creed mutters, more to himself than anyone else.

No one argues that point.

"Creed," I say, stepping closer. "Are we ready for what they bring?"

"Have to be," he replies, resolve hardening his features. "No other choice."

The moon hangs low, casting elongated shadows across the dirt. I glance around at my brothers, their faces set, minds already turning to defense, retribution, and survival.

And then there's Lyric. Her face flashes in my mind, innocent and unaware of how close the danger lurks. A pang of something fierce hits me.

Is it protection?

Fear?

Love?

I shove it down deep.

I can't afford that kind of distraction now, but it's there, smoldering like embers waiting to ignite.

"Highway." Creed's gaze locks onto mine, pulling me back. "You good?"

"Always," I lie.

The truth is, the thought of the Diablos cutting ties is a gut punch. The Royal Bastards is life, but without the deals, without the alliances...

Can we keep what we have?

Can we protect our own?

"Let's roll out," Creed commands, and we move as one, disappearing into the night.

As the roar of Harleys fills the void, my thoughts circle back to Lyric. I have to keep her safe—keep them all safe. If the Diablos are out, we're in for a hell of a ride. And I'll be damned if I let anything touch what's ours.

***

The roar of my Harley cuts through the quiet neighborhood as I pull up to Lyric's home. Gravel spits under the tires, scattering with a satisfying crunch. My heart hammers in my chest. This isn't a social call.

"Pack a bag," I bark the moment she opens the door. "You, too," I say to her father. "Clubhouse. Now."

Lyric's eyes flash with a mix of fear and excitement, but it's her dad who gets in my face. "Who the hell do you think—"

"It's dangerous for you and Lyric to be out here alone," I cut him off.

His gaze goes to Lyric, not Gwen. Not anymore.

It's the name that ties her to us, to me. To the Royal Bastards MC. His fight deflates, and his shoulders slump. He knows he's lost her to the life, to the chaos… to me.

"Five minutes," he grumbles, defeated.

"As fast as you can," I counter, the urgency clawing at my insides.

They hustle. Bags zip. Doors slam. The night is full of danger.

Lyric emerges, bag slung over her shoulder, looking like sin and salvation. She swings her leg over the back of my bike, pressing tight against me. Her arms snake around my waist, her grip steady. My heart kicks against my ribs. Yeah, this is right.

"Ready?" I ask, revving the engine.

"Yes," she whispers against my back, sending shivers down my spine.

I gun it down the road, leaving dust and

normalcy behind. Her father closely follows us in his Mercedes. The wind howls, blending with the bike's growl. It's us against the world now. Maybe, just maybe, we can carve out our own piece of forever—a wild, untamed, ride-or-die life.

Creed and Devil and Reaper and Lucy found their way through the fire. Maybe it's our turn now. As Lyric holds onto me, something fierce and tender wraps itself around my chest.

Yeah, we could be that unit. Solid. Unbreakable.

Against the rush of the night air and the pulse of the engine beneath us, I let myself believe we can make it.

The clubhouse looms ahead, a fortress against the encroaching darkness. The lot is crowded with bikes, chrome glinting under the security lights. Engines purr and rumble in a chorus that speaks of unity and power.

"Stay close," I mutter to Lyric as we dismount. Her nod, tight-lipped and determined, tells me she's all in. This is her world now too.

We push through the heavy door, the noise inside slamming into us like a physical force—laughter and shouts, the clinking of bottles. Life in the face of death. Creed has called church, and the room hums with anticipation. Everyone is here, bracing for whatever hell is about to break loose.

I scan the room. There are brothers with their arms around their women or their kids, making sure they've got a place to crash. Tension threads through the camaraderie. Eyes meet mine, and nods are exchanged. This is family. When shit hits the fan, it's the Royal Bastards who stand shoulder to shoulder.

"Food's on," a voice hollers from the kitchen, where club women are dishing out strength and comfort by the plateful. The smell of meat and spices fills the air, battling back the stink of fear.

Then she's there, Lucy, slicing through the crowd, her eyes locked on Lyric. Their sisterly bond is almost a lifeline I can literally see. She grabs Lyric's hand, and a silent conversation passes between them. They move toward the stairs. Her father follows, his face etched with worry and resignation. He looks back once, our eyes meeting. There's no blame there, just an unspoken understanding. He's entrusting me with another piece of his heart.

"Highway, I'm going to get Dad settled in the room across from yours and Lyric's," Lucy throws over her shoulder, not slowing down. They vanish upstairs, leaving me stranded in the storm.

"Fuck!" I exhale, watching them go. My room. Our room. A sanctuary for Lyric in this madhouse. She's under my skin, her name etched into my soul alongside the ink.

But there's no time for that now. I square my shoulders. There's war on the horizon, and every man here has a role to play. Mine is clear—I must protect, survive, and retaliate.

"Highway!" a voice calls, pulling me back to the present. Eyes on me, waiting.

"Yeah?" I say, my voice steady.

Time to plan our next move.

Time to show them who the Royal Bastards really are.

Leather creaks as I pivot, and the clubhouse feels alive. Feral is beside me, a shadow with rage in his eyes, muscles coiled tight. He jerks his head, and without a word, I follow him through the crowd, each step heavy with purpose.

We push open the door to the meeting room. Creed is at the table, his presence commanding silence. The leaders of our chapter flank him, faces grim. This is the inner sanctum where decisions are life or death.

"Betrayal." The word slams into the room from Creed's lips. "The Diablo Cartel. They've turned on us."

A collective growl ripples through the room, a sound that's all fury and no fear. My fists clench at my sides.

"Camilla," Feral spits the name like poison. "I'll tear her heart out. Make her regret the day she crossed the Royal Bastards."

"Ease up, brother." Creed's voice is calm but commanding. His gaze locks with Feral's. "That rage? Bottle it. We need cool heads, not just brute force. We need everyone we can count on to come out of this alive."

"Everyone?" I say, my voice low but cutting clear. "Even the Khans?"

"Every damn one of them." Creed's nod is slow and deliberate. "We're calling in every marker, every favor owed. This storm? We weather it together."

"United," someone mutters.

It's a pledge, a vow spoken in the language of the outlaw.

"United," the rest of us echo.

The Royal Bastards don't bend.

We sure as hell don't break.

Creed's voice slices through the murmurs, his eyes cold and calculating. "We hit them hard and hit them fast."

I nod, feeling that familiar surge of adrenaline— the rush that comes before the chaos. Every pair of eyes is fixed on Creed.

"Tonight," he says, and his words hang heavy, loaded. "We take the fight to them before they even smell the blood in the water."

A collective growl of approval ripples through us. We're predators, not prey. We set the traps but don't fall into them.

"Winchester," Creed's gaze cuts to where the man sits to his right. "We need to know the layout of the Crimson Wheelers' compound."

"Got it, Prez." Winchester's reply is a low rumble. "I've had it for a while."

"Good." Creed's lips twist into a half-smile that doesn't reach his eyes. "Let's remind the Wheelers who they're dealing with. And let the Diablo Cartel hear about it."

My hands curl into fists at my sides, knuckles itching for a fight. We're a brotherhood bound by blood and honor.

Betray us?

Hell hath no fury like the Royal Bastards scorned.

Creed's words echo in my head. Tonight, the streets will whisper our story—a tale of loyalty, retribution, and the fierce bond of the Royal Bastards MC.

Chapter 14

Highway

The world is a murky gray that messes with your head and makes you wonder if you're really awake or trapped in some twilight dream. I thumb the safety off my piece, the metallic click almost soothing against the distant hum of the early morning. We're an hour out from dawn.

"Stay sharp," Reaper whispers, his voice cutting through the silence.

My boots make almost no sound on the gravel, hushed and deliberate. This is the time when people are most likely lost in slumber—their guards are down and minds adrift. Dawn is perfect for a first strike.

Scanning the expanse of the Crimson Wheelers' compound, nothing stirs, but that doesn't mean squat. They could be lurking or waiting for us.

"Remember, no mistakes," Winchester says.

We know the stakes and risks, and we've all accepted them without hesitation. This isn't just a mission—it's personal.

"Keep the line open," I remind my brothers as I tap the earpiece I'm wearing because communication is our lifeline. One misstep could cost us everything, and I'm not about to let that happen. Not on my watch.

"Ready?" Reaper's question hangs in the air, heavy with the weight of what's to come.

Many of us nod.

The first glimmer of dawn bleeds into the sky. My heart hammers beneath my cut as we creep closer, our boots silent on the dew-slick grass.

We inch toward the compound's outer fence, the metallic scent of impending rain mingling with the adrenaline that courses through me. Each breath is a cloud of mist, each step a calculated risk.

"Positions," I signal, my fingers tight around the grip of my weapon. The others fan out, their forms blending into the half-light. We are the unseen, the unexpected.

With a nod, Reaper gives the signal. We surge forward, a wave of vengeance poised to crash upon those who wronged us. This is more than an attack—it's retribution.

We are the Royal Bastards, and this dawn

belongs to us.

Reaper turns his steely gaze to Fingers, who is clutching a laptop like it's his lifeline. "You make sure you bleed their computers dry. Everything they've got."

"Copy that," Fingers replies, pushing his glasses up the bridge of his nose. Though he's more at home behind a screen, the glint in his eyes says he's ready to throw down if necessary.

Winchester steps forward, pulling out a crumpled blueprint from his cut. Even in the dim light, I can see every mark, every notation he's made.

"Main entrance is a no-go, wired up the ass with cameras. We hit the side gate here..." He points. "Low surveillance, easy pickings."

"Escape routes?" I ask, scanning the layout.

"Back fence, over there..." he gestures off to the left, "... and a hidden passage through the garage."

"Good. Stay sharp, stay silent. We do this clean," Reaper commands. "Let's carve 'em up." Reaper smirks, the threat in his tone unmistakable.

Justice slinks ahead, a shadow among shadows. He moves like he's part cat. I watch him dismantle an alarm with a few deft flicks of his wrist, his fingers steady as a surgeon's.

"Clear," he whispers, barely a breath on the wind.

"Copy that," I reply, my voice just as low.

We edge closer to the compound with every muscle coiled tight, ready for what's next. My heart drums against my ribs, but it's not fear—it's the thrill of the hunt.

I signal the rest of the Bastards with a swift hand motion, and like the ghostly riders of legend, we advance, unseen, unheard, and unstoppable.

"Stay sharp," I murmur, my voice cutting through the hush. "Keep your heads on a swivel and your comms open. We're not out for a Sunday ride... this is the real deal."

"Roger that, Highway," comes the static-laced reply over the earpieces. A chorus of agreement ripples through the group.

"Justice, Winchester, you're up," Reaper says through the comms.

They slip away from the group with practiced ease, their movements fluid and silent as they position themselves.

Winchester crouches by a cluster of bushes, his broad frame surprisingly stealthy. His eyes are on the main gate, fingers flexing around the grip of his weapon, ready to unleash hell if need be.

"Winchester's set," he confirms, his tone low, barely above a whisper, yet clear as day in my ear.

"Good. Justice?" I prompt, knowing full well the man can hear me.

"I'm good to go," Justice replies, and even though I can't see him, I can picture the smirk on his face.

"Let's show 'em how the Bastards party," Reaper growls.

And with that, we move, a single entity driven by purpose and the unbreakable bonds of brotherhood. The hunt is on.

Reaper's signal cuts through the haze, a clenched fist raised high. No more waiting, no more schemes. It's go-time.

My hand tightens around my piece. Adrenaline pumps through my veins. This is what we bleed for—the rush of the ride, the fight, the brotherhood. Fingers is right beside me, a silent shadow that knows tonight is not just about muscle—it's about intel.

Metal clanks and chains snap. We're through the gate, storming the inner sanctum of the enemy. With Justice's handiwork, all the security systems are down before they knew what hit them.

"Let's light 'em up," someone yells, and the morning explodes into chaos.

"Taking point," Winchester's voice crackles through, calm amidst the chaos.

"Flank secured," Justice confirms, just as steady.

Gunfire erupts, bullets singing a deadly lullaby. We move together, fluid and relentless. The Crimson Wheelers scramble, caught off guard by our early-morning strike.

We're inside now, tearing through their defenses.

It's mayhem.

It's madness.

It's a Royal Bastards' raid in all its glory.

The compound is ours, room by room, hall by hall. Their resistance crumbles beneath our onslaught. Winchester and Justice hold fast outside, keeping any would-be heroes from interrupting us.

Fingers moves into a room that has a computer with me keeping watch.

"Crimson Wheelers' secrets will soon be ours," Fingers states as he hacks away while I lay down cover.

I'm perched behind an old couch and an upturned table, my eyes fixed on Fingers as he frantically types away on a battered laptop. The staccato clack of keys blends with the relentless chatter of gunfire. I squeeze the trigger once, twice, sending Crimson Wheelers to the floor, their bodies crumpling like rag dolls.

"Cover me, Highway!" Fingers shouts without looking up, his fingers dancing across the keyboard.

"Got your back," I reply, reloading in a flash.

My hands are steady, even as adrenaline pumps through my veins. Another Wheeler pops out from behind a door, but he's met with a bullet that sends him spiraling backward.

A Royal Bastard never stands alone. That's our creed. To my left, Feral lays down a curtain of bullets, his face an impassive mask as he kills anyone who dares to oppose us.

"Highway, three o'clock!" Winchester's voice cuts through the sound of screams and gunfire.

I pivot, sighting down my barrel. Three Wheelers think they've got the drop on us. They're wrong. My finger hugs the trigger, and three shots ring out. The first man staggers forward, a trickle of blood moving down his face as dead eyes stare at me. The second howls in pain, clutching his chest, and then he falls. The last man falls backward, eyes and mouth open as though he can't believe he got out-gunned.

"Nice shooting." Winchester smirks, reloading his weapon. His eyes are alight with the thrill of the fight, a predator in his element.

We move as one, the Royal Bastards, fueled by the need to protect our own. I watch as one of us takes a hit, goes down, but not out. Tank, built like the machine he's named after, is back on his feet in seconds, bloodied but unbowed. His roar is feral as he charges, taking the fight to the enemy.

Right now, we're ensuring it's the Crimson Wheelers who taste death.

"Done," Fingers exclaims triumphantly.

He snaps the laptop shut and slides it into his bag with one hand while firing off a few rounds with the other.

"Time to blow this joint," I declare, signaling the retreat with a sharp whistle.

I'm a shadow behind Reaper. He's a damn force of nature, barreling through the Crimson Wheelers with nothing but muscle and steel. I watch, almost in awe, as he grabs a rival by the collar, headbutting him hard enough to send him sprawling.

"Should've stayed down," Reaper growls out as the guy tries to crawl away.

This one's trying to beg, blood bubbling from his split lip. Reaper doesn't hesitate. His knife flashes, a silver streak in the dim light, and then there's silence. It's quick, clean, and surgical.

"Damn," I mutter under my breath.

Two more try their luck, rushing him like that's going to save them. Reaper sidesteps the first and sends him crashing into the second. They're entangled, confusion etched on their faces. Reaper's boot meets a ribcage, and there's a crunch that has me wincing.

"Pathetic," Reaper spits out.

His blade finds flesh again and again. No shots are fired, just the slick sound of a knife cutting life short. Two thuds, bodies hitting the floor. Reaper stands, chest heaving, drenched in the proof of his kills.

"Good thing you're with us," I say, clapping him on the back.

Reaper only nods, his eyes already scanning for the next threat.

The survivors are herded inside the clubhouse,

like cattle to the slaughter. The air is thick with fear and gun smoke, walls echoing with the ghosts of their fallen brothers.

"Talk," Reaper commands, his voice deadly calm. He's got this way of speaking that chills you to the bone.

One by one, they will spill their guts, hoping for mercy. Reaper's knife glints in his hand, a silent judge.

"Diablo Cartel?" he asks the first, who is shaking so bad his teeth chatter.

"Money... they paid for protection," the Wheeler stammers, eyes darting around, seeking an escape that isn't there.

Reaper nods, and it's over before the guy can blink. Next, next, and next—each confession sealed with a final slice.

"Last one," Reaper says, almost bored.

The last Wheeler is crying now, snot and tears mixing with the dirt on his face. "Please," he whimpers.

"Did you think you stood a chance?" Reaper's voice is a whisper of death.

The guy looks directly at me and gasps just before Reaper's knife ends the conversation for good.

All five are gone.

The questions hang in the air, unanswered whispers drowned in blood.

Without being told, I pour gasoline over the bodies. The smell of it clings to my hands, a pungent reminder of the task at hand. I douse the buildings as well, the liquid splashing over wooden floors and lifeless faces, erasing their identities as easily as we snuffed out their lives. My boots soak up the fuel as I walk, leaving dark, wet prints on the wooden floor.

"What about the women?" I ask Reaper.

There are a few of them huddled together at the back of the clubhouse. Reaper shrugs, but I'm not about to kill females who didn't join in the fight or can't look after themselves.

"We could let them go?"

Slowly, Reaper shakes his head from side to side. The blood of his enemies covers most of him, making him appear more monster than man.

"W-We won't say anything," one of the women says as she steps forward.

One of her friends grabs her hand and tries to pull her back into the group.

"Some of us didn't want to be here in the first place." She glances over her shoulder at a girl who could be more than fifteen, then stares at me. "*Please.*"

Reaper tilts his head to the side, studying her. "I know you."

She nods. "I was Hawk's sister."

Reaper's eyebrows shoot up. "Thought you were

dead. Jet, yeah?"

"Yeah, and I might as well have been." Jet looks around at the dead men on the floor.

Justice walks into the room, and Reaper gives him a chin lift. "Get them all back to our clubhouse."

Jet takes another step forward. "I'm not trading this life for another shitty one with the likes of you." Her eyes blaze with defiance.

Reaper laughs. "I don't take sloppy seconds, and you won't be. We just need to make sure we're all on the same page, and after a reasonable amount of time, you can all leave."

Justice moves forward, and she cocks her head to the side. Whatever he sees in her eyes causes him to stop.

"Give me your word we won't be used like whores or slaves or whatever the fuck your gang does."

Reaper laughs and points his knife at Jet. "I like you. You've got balls." The smile falls off his face, and he moves right into her personal space.

I wince inwardly, knowing if it were me, I'd back down, but damn if this woman doesn't have a spine. Jet doesn't step back, and she stares Reaper in the eyes. They stay locked like that until one of the other women lets out a sob. Reaper stares past Jet, then nods.

"You have my word. No one will hurt you, but

you will come to our compound. This is non-negotiable."

Jet steps back and nods. "I'm going to hold you to that."

Reaper quirks an eyebrow at her. "Time to go."

Justice steps forward. "Ladies, if you'll all follow me?"

Jet puts her arm around the young girl, and they follow Justice out.

"You did the right thing," I say to Reaper.

He shrugs. "Make it rain, Highway," Reaper says, his voice an undercurrent of darkness in the silence that follows death.

I pull the matches from my pocket, striking one against the rough side of the box. The flame flickers to life, small and insignificant against the carnage around us. But its power lies in what comes next. I flick the match into the pooling gasoline, a simple gesture that ignites an inferno.

Flames roar to life, greedy tongues licking up the sides of the clubhouse. Heat washes over me, and for a moment, I feel like the devil himself. The fire devours everything, consuming the evidence of our retribution with hungry fervor. Crimson Wheelers, their clubhouse, their secrets—all of it turns to ash and smoke under the wrath of the Royal Bastards.

"Let's ride," I call out, my voice hoarse but steady.

There's nothing left here for us but echoes and embers.

***

The rumble of my bike is a familiar comfort as we ride back to our territory, the morning air washing the stench of blood and gasoline from my nostrils. I can't wait to see Lyric, to feel something other than the adrenaline and cold resolve that's been my companion.

The Royal Bastards' clubhouse comes into view, and my heart kicks up a notch.

Home.

Safety.

Lyric.

She's there before I even kill the engine, rushing out to meet me. My Lyric with her wild hair and eyes that have seen too much but still shine when they look at me. She throws herself into my arms, and I hold her tight, breathing in the scent of her shampoo, a stark contrast to the smell of destruction lingering on my clothes.

"Highway," she whispers—it soothes the jagged edges inside me.

"Lyric," I respond, my lips finding hers in a kiss that speaks of the fear, loss, and the relief of return. It's soft and fierce all at once, a promise and a homecoming.

"Are you okay?" she asks, pulling back just enough to search my face with worried eyes.

"Better now," I admit, meaning every damn word.

Her touch is warmth and life, a reminder of why we fight so hard and cling to this brotherhood of outcasts and warriors.

"Come on," she murmurs, taking my hand.

"Not yet."

Her eyebrows come together in a frown, but she lets me pull her toward the bonfire burning at the back of the clubhouse. I take off all my clothing and boots, then throw them into the flames. There will be no forensic evidence to link us to the carnage at the Crimson Wheelers' compound.

One by one, all the men who were at the raid do the same. Tank stands next to me, blood oozing down his chest as he stares into the flames.

"You okay, brother?"

He doesn't look at me. "Yeah. This is only the beginning, isn't it?"

Glancing at Lyric, I nod. "Yeah."

She puts her hand in mind and pulls me through the clubhouse. Lyric asks no questions, and I feel as long as she's by my side, I've got something worth returning to. No matter what hell we ride through, Lyric is my haven, and for her, I'd burn down the world or build it anew.

The clubhouse is silent as we each retreat into

our rooms, looking for a shower and clean clothes. Lyric turns on the faucet, and I step under the spray, letting the water wash me clean. There's a knock on the door, and she leaves me to see who it is, only to come back a few moments later.

"Winchester said to give you this?" Lyric looks puzzled as she hands me a bottle of bleach.

"He's making sure none of us goes down for what we did."

Using a scrub brush, I pour the bleach on myself and scour my skin. It flushes red, and I don't stop until the whole bottle has been used. The water goes cold long before I'm finished. When I'm done, I step out onto the tiled floor, and Lyric wraps me in a towel.

"Do you want to talk about it?"

"Creed will be waiting for us."

"Will you talk about it?"

The atmosphere feels heavy with the weight of unspoken truths. My rough exterior hides a tumultuous past, and the broad-shouldered frame I carry feels burdened by countless dark deeds.

I run a hand through my tousled hair, a nervous gesture that contrasts with my usual composed demeanor. Taking a deep breath, my chest rises and falls heavily as if preparing myself for the weight of my confessions.

"Yes."

Lyric steps closer, touching my hand, gentle yet

reassuring. In that moment, I realize that sharing my darkness will not drive her away but bring us closer. For the first time, I feel the possibility of redemption and the hope that true and unwavering love can heal even the deepest wounds.

She kisses me and entwines her fingers in my hair, then steps back, her nose wrinkling. "You smell like bleach."

Grinning, I say, "I smell clean."

"Are you hungry?" Lyric asks.

"Yeah." It feels like forever since I last ate.

"I'll make you a plate and have it upstairs waiting for you." She goes up on her tiptoes and presses her lips to mine before disappearing downstairs.

***

Creed sits at the head of the table, his eyes scanning each of us as we stride in one by one. The tension in his shoulders eases when his gaze lands on Reaper, Fingers, and me. We're battered but alive.

"Report," Creed commands, his voice carrying the weight of authority and unspoken concern.

Reaper steps forward, his knuckles once stained red are now scrubbed and clean, much like my own. "Crimson Wheelers' clubhouse is ashes. Casualties on their side were extensive. We lost no one."

"Good." Creed nods once, sharp and decisive. He turns to Fingers, who is already flipping open his laptop, the screen casting a pale glow on his concentrated face. "What have you got?"

Fingers doesn't look up, his fingers flying over the keys. "It's just like we thought, Creed. The money trail's as dirty as they come. Shell companies and backdoor deals. But it's clear as day, Diablo Cartel's stink is all over the Crimson Wheelers."

"Show me," Creed demands.

I lean against the wall, arms crossed, watching the screen come to life, a damning picture of betrayal and corruption. Numbers and transfers, dates and times, all weaving a narrative we'd suspected but can now confirm.

"Here." Fingers points at a cluster of transactions. "Payments made days before the rally. And here..." his finger jabs at another series of entries "... more payouts, scheduled for after. They wanted to squeeze us out, take control."

Creed's jaw clenches, eyes flinty with the cold rage that promises retribution. "Diablo Cartel is gonna regret crossing the Royal Bastards."

A murmur of agreement ripples through the room. We're more than a club. We are a family. And when one of us is threatened, we all stand ready to ride into hell together.

"Anything else?" Creed's stare pins Fingers down, demanding every last detail.

"That's the bulk of it," Fingers replies, shutting his laptop with a snap. "But I'll keep digging.

There's always more dirt to find."

"Good man." Creed's praise is rare, making it all the more valuable. He surveys the room again. "We'll need all the intel we can get. The Diablos have deep pockets, but they just bought themselves a war they won't walk away from."

There's a deadly promise in Creed's voice. We're the Royal Bastards, and don't bow down to anyone.

"Everyone but Highway, Winchester, Reaper, and Justice... *out*," Creed commands

The room clears, leaving us four, Creed's trusted council. He fishes a cell from his cut, thumbing it with a fury I recognize all too well.

"Camilla," he barks into the speakerphone, the name like a bullet. "Why?"

Her laugh crackles through the silence, high and mocking. "You Royal Bastards are merely pawns," she sneers. "Pawns in the Diablos' game."

Creed's face reddens, muscles twitching with barely contained rage. "After all these years..." he starts, his voice low and dangerous.

"Your loyalty was your downfall," Camilla interrupts, her tone icy. "The Crimson Wheelers will finish you soon enough."

Silence descends for a heartbeat before Creed's laughter—a cold, mirthless sound—fills the room. "You think you've got us cornered?" His gaze meets mine, fiery and resolute. "The Crimson Wheelers are dead. Jacksonville is ours. Never underestimate a Royal Bastard."

The line goes dead.

Silence hangs heavy, charged with the weight of impending war. But as I look around at my brothers, at Creed, who is unyielding, I feel it—the unbreakable bond.

Creed slams his fist down on the table, his jaw set, eyes like flint. He doesn't skip a beat, punching in another number. His calloused finger presses the final digit, and he switches the phone to speaker for everyone to hear.

"Da." The voice on the other end cuts through, heavy with a Russian accent.

"Creed for Lev," he growls into the silence, every word a promise of retribution.

The room is thick with tension and charged with electricity. I can almost taste the violence in the air, feel it pulsing in my veins. We're standing at the edge of an abyss—war with the Diablos—and we're about to jump.

"Da?"

"Lev." Creed's voice is steel wrapped in velvet, a dangerous combination that means business.

"It is early," replies the Russian.

"He will want to speak with me. Tell him who it is."

"Lev's not gonna like this," the Russian on the other end mutters, but there's a current of curiosity under the annoyance.

"Lev will want to hear this," Creed insists, his tone brokering no argument. "It's about the Diablos."

The line is quiet for a heartbeat, just the crackle of anticipation. Then a rustle, like someone's being roused from sleep—the sound of murmuring, the shuffle of movement, followed by a click as if a door closes somewhere far away.

"Speak," a new voice commands, thick with authority and the remnants of disrupted dreams.

Creed leans in, his eyes narrow slits of calculation. "I've got a proposition that'll benefit us both. It's time to push the Diablo Cartel out of Jacksonville."

"Yes?" Lev's interest piques, almost tangible across the wire.

"Yes," Creed confirms, a ghost of a smirk flickering across his lips. "We take them down, and we share the throne. You in?"

Silence stretches taut between them. Every second ticking by has my heart pounding in my chest. Reaper's fingers twitch beside his blade, and Winchester's stoic gaze is locked on Creed.

"Is this your move, Royal Bastard?" The title isn't mockery but recognition.

"Checkmate." Creed's voice is a promise.

"Interesting." Lev's voice is a growl of approval. "You have my attention. Let's talk."

Creed nods once, sharp and decisive. He glances

at us, his warriors, his brothers. We're in this together, each of us ready to ride through Hell's flames.

"Good," he says. "Because when the Royal Bastards make a move, we play to win."

"You've finally had enough of the Diablos, my friend?"

"Enough to make a deal."

Lev chuckles, the sound like breaking glass. "And what makes you think we would align with the Royal Bastards?"

"Common enemy," Creed shoots back.

"Ah, so it is war you're preparing for." He's not asking but confirming what he already knows.

"War's already here," Creed says, scanning the room. Reaper, Winchester, and Justice are all stone-faced and ready. "Just picking sides now."

"Ha!" He barks, a single, mirthless laugh. "Tell me your terms, Creed."

"Simple…" Creed presses on, "Your muscle, your reach. In return, we carve up Jacksonville. Diablo Cartel gets the boot."

"Generous offer," Lev muses, the line humming with the weight of his consideration.

"Smart business," Creed counters. "You get a slice of the South without dirtying your hands too much."

"Yes, you have a point," Lev concedes.

"Listen." Creed leans in. "We've been

underestimating each other. Time to correct that mistake."

"Underestimation can be deadly, yes," Lev agrees, a note of respect threading through his words.

"Then let's make them pay," Creed urges

"Perhaps," Lev drawls, dragging out the moment, savoring the power he holds. But I can tell he's hooked, intrigued by the chaos we propose.

"Back us, and we'll push the Diablo Cartel out of Jacksonville. Together."

"Bold, Creed, very bold." Lev's voice drops an octave, a sign he's in. "All right. You have my support."

"Good."

"This will be interesting."

"Interesting enough to shake up the whole damn city," Creed promises, clenching the phone.

"Very well," Lev says, sealing the deal with two words.

"Talk soon, Lev." Creed hangs up before he can reply.

We've just struck a deal with the devil himself.

And hell, if it isn't exactly where the Royal Bastards thrive.

Chapter 15

Lyric

I'm slicing tomatoes when Dad bursts through the kitchen door like a storm. His face is tight, eyes hard with that look he gets when life's gone sideways after an operation gone wrong.

"Gwen," he pants, his voice edged with something that sounds like fear.

"Hey, what's wrong?" I ask, dropping the knife, my heart kicking up a notch.

He's never this rattled. Dad is a plastic surgeon, and there's not much he hasn't seen.

His gaze sweeps the room, landing on me like a physical touch. "Those women…" he starts, and there's a tremor in his hands that doesn't belong, "… the ones your *friends* brought in."

I swallow and wipe my hands on my jeans, feeling the weight of his stare. "Yes?" I prod, trying to keep my tone level.

"One's just a kid, Gwen." He's at my side now. "Fifteen, maybe. She's... God." He is gripping the counter like it's the only thing keeping him up. "She's been..."

I don't need him to finish. My stomach twists into a hard knot, and I feel the color drain from my face.

"Beaten? Raped?" The words taste like bile.

"Both," he confirms, and the simple word is a punch to the gut.

"Jesus, Dad..." I reach out and touch his arm, trying to ground us both.

"Can't let this stand," he mutters, looking past me now toward the phone—toward calling in the cavalry that can't come.

"Wait, Dad." I catch his eye. "Trust me, okay? Just... trust me."

He nods once, sharp and tight. But I see it in his eyes, the battle he's fighting to do his job or to be my father. It's tearing him up inside.

"All right, *Lyric*." My club name sounds rough. "But you better have a damn good plan."

I nod because I have to, but there's no other choice, and when Highway trusts you with something, you don't let it fall apart. Not if you can help it.

"Got it, Dad. We'll fix this... somehow. You can't call the police, Dad," I say without preamble. "Please trust us, trust me."

"Gwen, these women—" he starts, anxiety etching deeper lines into his face.

"Trust," I repeat, locking eyes with him.

He nods, but I can tell he's not convinced. Dad goes back the way he came, and I stride out of the kitchen, my heart hammering against my chest. I'm searching for Lucy and find her standing with Justice. She's listening to him speak out near the bonfire.

They turn to me as I approach.

Justice's jaw is set, a muscle ticking there as he speaks, "Reaper gave his word they'd be okay, but we can't risk them talking. Not after what they saw."

"Damn Crimson Wheelers," Lucy mutters, her voice low and dangerous.

"Exactly. They've seen too much. We need to be sure they won't go running to the cops."

"You're talking about the women? Dad just said one of them, she's only fifteen, has been raped and beaten."

Once upon a time, I was out there, camera in hand, capturing life at its rawest. Now, here I am, caught up in the gritty reality of the Royal Bastards, where loyalty runs deeper than blood.

I glance back at the clubhouse, its walls holding secrets and safety—my new home. There's no way they would harm those women.

But what's the next move?

A shiver runs through me, not from fear but from the unknown.

What will we do with them?

How do we prove to the women that we're not the monsters they think we are?

"Lyric," Lucy calls out, pulling me back to the moment. "We'll figure this out. Together."

Justice nods, and I do, too, but I can't help but think those women have no reason to trust us. We've kidnapped them from one MC to another. How do I get them to keep the Royal Bastards' secrets? Can they ever leave the MC?

Lucy grabs my hand, and we weave through the crowded clubhouse, our steps quick and purposeful. Dad is in the infirmary, his face drawn with concern, his doctor's hands steady as they tend to the wounded. The air is thick with antiseptic and fear.

"Dad, can we help?"

His gaze flickers over to Jet, who stands like a bruised sentinel at the edge of the room. Her defiance is tangible, a shield she wields fiercely.

"I could use some bottled water and food for these women." He looks up at the ceiling, then back at us. "They could use showers and clean clothes."

Justice steps into the threshold, his frame filling the doorway. "Anything I can do?"

"Get out!" Jet's voice spits, her distrust a palpable force pushing against Justice's solid presence.

He raises his hands in a gesture of peace and backs away.

"Let's find Highway," I mutter to Lucy, and she nods, understanding.

The kitchen is empty, save for the hum of the refrigerator. I gather up bread, cold cuts, and a knife. My hands move automatically, assembling a sandwich with practiced ease. Food always tastes better after chaos. I learned that in Afghanistan.

"Highway?" I call out softly, stepping into the dim hallway that leads to our room.

A shadow moves, and then he's there, his presence calming the storm inside me.

"Hey, Lyric," he greets, the corner of his mouth lifting in that familiar half-smile.

"Made you something to eat," I say, leading him back to our sanctuary.

Once inside, I hand him the plate and sit close, needing the warmth of his body, the certainty of his strength.

"Talk to me. What happened at the Crimson Wheelers' compound?"

He takes a bite, chews thoughtfully, then meets my gaze. "They're done. No more threats from that corner of the world."

"Dead," I whisper, and he nods once, confirming the finality of it all.

"And the women?" I ask, my heart hammering with the weight of what's to come.

"They're safe, Lyric. As long as the Diablos are kept at bay and the cops aren't sniffing around, they'll be free to go."

"Promise?" The word hangs between us.

"Promise," he replies, wrapping an arm around me and pulling me in closer.

"Thanks, Highway," I breathe out, relief mingling with worry, my mind already racing ahead to the next battle.

I press my lips to Highway's in a quick, fierce kiss. "Be right back," I murmur against his mouth, then slip away before he can pull me back.

The hallway is thick with people, but I navigate through them and reach the door where the women are located. I knock twice, softly, and push it open.

Inside, the smell of antiseptic stings my nostrils. My father, whose face is pinched with concern, hovers over a girl lying on a bed.

"This is Mia," Dad says with a smile.

The girl looks up at me, and she must be the fifteen-year-old. Her eyes are too old for her face. Her back is a mess of angry red welts. My stomach clenches as bile rises.

"Hey, Mia," I say gently, kneeling beside her. "You're safe now, okay? You're with us."

"Am I?" she whispers, her voice barely there.

"Yes," I insist, brushing a strand of hair from her damp forehead.

"Can I have a phone?" Jet's voice cuts through the

thick air. She stands in the corner, arms wrapped around herself like she's holding herself together.

"Why?" I ask.

"I need to call my mom," she says, a tremble in her voice. "Been almost a year since—"

"Since what, Jet?" I prod.

"Since Hawk died," she blurts out. "My brother. He was friends with Reaper and wanted to be in the Royal Bastards till a bullet ended that dream."

"Jesus…" I whisper.

"Didn't know MCs saw women as nothing, but…" She doesn't finish.

"The Royal Bastards aren't like that," I say. "They protect their own."

"Can I leave then?" Jet challenges, her eyes sparking with rebellion.

"Gwen…" Dad's warning tone slices through the tension. "They were forced here."

"Doesn't feel safe," Jet spits, disbelief etched in every line of her face. "Feels like a cage."

"Trust me," I plead, my heart a drumbeat in my chest. "We're the good guys."

Jet just stares, her gaze loaded with doubt. The tension in the room is so thick it's like trying to breathe through a wet blanket.

Lucy bursts in, her eyes scanning the scene. "You're not prisoners. Diablos could be on your tails if you step out," she adds, but there's a softness there, too, a crack in her tough-girl façade.

That's when Devil struts into the chaos, that wild Aussie spark in her eyes. "No need to be worried about nothing, loves." She chuckles, waving off the concern with a flick of her wrist. "If you want to leave, door's open. But trust me, this is the safest bloody place for you." She turns to Jet. "Come shopping with me? We need food and clothes for you lot."

Jet's eyes narrow suspiciously. "What's the catch?"

Devil giggles, a sound that seems too carefree for this heavy room. "No catch. Just help me pick the stuff and carry it back. Yes?"

Before anyone can process that, Justice swings in, all swagger and smirks. "Ready, Devil?" he asks, his gaze locking on Jet.

"Are we?" Devil echoes, challenging.

Jet hesitates, then shakes her head slightly, but not in refusal. It's more like she's shaking off her doubts.

Justice leans in, his grin wicked. "Don't tell me you're scared," he teases, and I can see the interest sparking in his eyes.

Jet straightens up, her spine steeling. She might be wounded, but she's no damsel. "Never," she fires back, and there's a flash of the girl she must've been before all this.

And just like that, we're a convoy of unlikely allies.

Devil leads the way, Justice at her side, and Jet sandwiched between them. I fall in behind, my heart hammering a rhythm of anticipation. Devil climbs into the driver's seat of an SUV and Justice into the front passenger seat, which leaves the back seat for Jet and me and we drive.

The Walmart parking lot is a concrete sea of people rushing to and from the building's entrance. Justice climbs out of the SUV and opens the door for Jet with a flourish.

"Ma'am," he drawls as she gets out.

She frowns up at him, unimpressed. "You're all about chivalry?"

"Sometimes," Justice counters with a lazy grin, leaning against the frame. "Just being neighborly."

"Neighborly?" She scoffs, a harsh laugh escaping her lips. "There's no such thing." She brushes past him.

"Oi!" Devil's voice cuts through the tension like a whipcrack. "Eyes peeled, Justice. We're not here for a bloody picnic." She throws a pointed look my way. "In and out, yeah?"

"Got it, boss lady," Justice mutters, but there's a glint of respect in his eyes as he slams the door shut behind Jet.

We navigate inside the huge Walmart with Devil leading the way.

"Stay close," I whisper to Jet, watching her survey the aisles like they're enemy territory.

"Thought this was supposed to be safe," she mutters back, even though her gaze keeps darting to the entrance where more of our guys have taken up posts.

"Appearances can be deceiving," I say, but my words feel hollow.

How do I explain that these men, who look like they could cause a riot with a single word, are really here to protect us?

"Looks like a damn guard detail," Jet observes, her tone edged with suspicion.

"Protection, not prison," I assure her, but the skepticism in her eyes doesn't fade.

It's Devil who changes the tune, her laughter bouncing off the shelves. "Relax, love! They're just making sure no one messes with our discount deals." She snags a bright red cart and starts loading it with food like we're stocking up for an apocalypse.

Jet watches, still bristling with wariness, but I can see the edges of her resolve softening. Maybe it's how Devil cracks jokes with those around her or how she tosses a bag of cookies into the cart, declaring them essential for mental health.

"See," I nudge Jet, gesturing at Devil's easy demeanor. "Not all MCs run like the one you were in."

She doesn't respond but follows Devil's whirlwind energy, her eyes slowly absorbing the scene. It's when our brothers step aside for an Ol' Lady, nodding with something like reverence, that I see the flicker of realization in Jet's eyes.

"Maybe," she concedes, the word almost lost beneath the store's tinny music.

Devil pushes the cart at Justice. "Go on and start ringing this up. I'm taking the girls on a trip through the clothing aisles."

"Devil, Creed will have my balls in a glass jar if anything happens to you."

Devil laughs. "We'll be fine." She opens her jacket to reveal a gun in its holster. "This was a present from Winchester, and he showed me how to use it. Now, go."

She is already walking away from him to get another cart. He looks at Jet and me briefly, shakes his head, and moves toward the checkout.

Devil links one arm with Jet and pushes the cart with the other. "Okay, you know your friends better than we do. They'll need at least two sets of clothes with underwear, so let's get shopping."

"What do I pick?"

Devil picks up a pink tank top and holds it against herself. "Whatever you think they will be most comfortable in." She tosses the tank into the cart.

Jet takes a tentative step forward and looks at the jeans. "I'm not sure of sizes."

"Best guess will do." Devil holds up a pair of

jeans to Jet. "Do you like skinny jeans?"

"Ahh, no. I like bootleg."

Devil nudges her. "Me, too, but Creed likes skinny jeans."

Jet looks down at Devil's bootleg jeans. "But you're not wearing those."

Devil waves a hand in the air as she picks up another pair of jeans. "Girl, of course not." She smiles at Jet. "But I do wear them on date night."

"Date night?"

"We're married, not dead. Yeah, date night."

Jet looks from me to Devil. "I don't understand."

Moving forward, I pick up a shirt off the rack. "What don't you understand?"

"She's wearing bootleg jeans, and she's going on dates with the biker who claimed her."

Devil frowns, her normally sunny disposition fading a little. "Honey, Creed and I are a couple. We fight, we make up, but he doesn't own me. I love Creed, and he loves me."

Jet's eyes widen, but she says nothing.

"I really like Highway."

Devil laughs at me. "I think that boy more than likes you."

"Wait. You're not forced to be there? You can leave?"

"Yes. And as soon as they think it's safe for you, you can leave too. Now, let's get picking clothes. It looks like Justice is finished ringing up the groceries, so he's going to be back any second. He'll be bitching and moaning we're taking too long." Devil begins throwing tank tops into the cart, then stops and looks at Jet. "Do you need shoes?"

Jet looks down at her worn-out sneakers. "Could I have boots?"

Devil grins. "Sure, if they've got them."

Jet returns her smile, and it lights up her whole face.

By the time we're finished, there's shoes, underwear, and more than two sets of clothes for everyone, but Devil keeps insisting no one will mind.

***

We arrive back at the clubhouse. It echoes with the growl of bikes and the distant clash of beer bottles. Devil's strides are purposeful as she rounds the SUV, her eyes glinting with mischief. She hands Jet a cell phone.

"Call your mum, love," she says, her Aussie accent wrapping around the words.

Jet's fingers tremble as they wrap around the phone, her tough façade cracking like pavement under a sledgehammer. Tears well up, spilling over, and she blinks hard—once, twice—before they cascade down her cheeks.

"Wh-why?" Jet stammers, her voice a broken whisper.

"Because family's everything," Devil replies. Her smile softens as she wraps an arm around Jet.

Justice moves in, his presence a solid reassurance. He lays a hand on Jet's shoulder, gently, nothing like the hard grips I've seen him use in fights.

"Let it out. It's okay," he murmurs, his voice a low rumble as comforting as a warm blanket on a cold night.

Jet looks at him, her confusion raw and open. "But you... you're one of them."

"Doesn't mean I'm not human," Justice counters, his eyes locking onto hers.

I watch from the sidelines, my heart caught somewhere between pride and something else for the man who stands with us.

"Go on, then." Devil nudges Jet gently. "Before your tears short-circuit the bloody thing."

A small laugh hiccups through Jet's sobs, and I can't help but grin. Devil has a way about her that can turn a storm into a drizzle.

With shaking hands, Jet dials, each beep a step closer to a world she's been torn from for too long. The call connects, and her voice is a quiet murmur, words meant only for the person on the other side of the line.

"Mom? It's me... Jet."

Something inside me eases as I watch her, this girl who's seen too much darkness finding a sliver of light. And Justice, this brute of a man with a heart bigger than his biceps, stands by her, unwavering.

I leave them to their moment, stepping quietly away, my boots echoing softly on the gravel driveway. I keep going through the clubhouse and upstairs. The door to our room creaks open, revealing Highway stretched out on the bed, his chest rising and falling with the deep, even breaths of sleep.

Creeping in, I toe off my boots and slide under the covers beside him, careful not to wake him. His warmth seeps into me.

In the quiet of our room, with Highway's steady breathing for company, I let my mind wander back to Jet, Justice, and the strange, twisted family we've become.

Outside, the world might be gunning for us, danger lurking in every shadow.

But here, now, there's peace and hope.

And maybe, just maybe, that's enough to keep the darkness at bay.

***

The stillness of the night is a lie.

My eyes snap open, my heart hammering against my ribcage, the afterimage of dreams fading fast.

Darkness wraps around me like a shroud, but I'm alert now, senses sharp as shattered glass.

"Trouble's brewing," I murmur, words barely a whisper in the charged air.

Highway stirs beside me. "Bad dream?" he grunts, his voice gravelly with sleep.

"Yeah." I slide out from under the covers, my feet planted firmly on the cold floor.

"Come back to bed. I'll chase your demons away." A dark promise is in his tone as he sits up, muscles coiling.

"Not sure I can sleep."

"Then we can play," Highway teases.

Shaking my head, I say, "You ever feel tired and awake at the same time?" I lay back down next to him.

"Yes." Highway nods, the shadow of a smile on his face.

"Do I need to worry about the Diablos?"

He turns and brushes a few strands of hair off my face. "Creed has a plan. Trust in him, and you'll be safe while you're here. I promise."

Highway pulls me in closer, his arms wrap around me, and I drift off to sleep in the safety of his arms.

Chapter 16

Highway

Dawn barely breaks, the world outside still clinging to the night. Lyric is nestled beside me, and I absently run my hand up and down her back. She stirs and looks around the room.

"What time is it?"

"Dawn." I point at the window above our heads. "You can see the sun's rays streaking across the sky."

"Why are you awake?"

"Creed will want to see us all. There's work to be done, and I've slept enough."

Lyric moves and places her chin on my chest, a frown creasing her pretty face. "Does that mean you'll be busy all day?"

"Probably, but I'll check in on you from time to time."

A smile transforms her face into a thing of beauty. "I'd like that."

"What are you going to do today?"

"Help Dad in the infirmary with the women. He's still not sure about keeping them here, and I need to reassure him that here is the safest place for them."

Lyric turns over and sits up, putting her feet on the floor.

"You could sleep in," I offer.

"With so many people in the clubhouse, I think I should go help with breakfast."

I move to sit beside her, and my heart warms that she's thinking about the MC and not herself.

"We'll catch up later?"

"Yeah."

Leaning in, I close the distance between us. Our lips meet, a soft, gentle touch at first, tentative and tender. The kiss deepens, her lips parting slightly as our breaths mingle. It's not perfect—there's the undeniable reality of morning breath—but it doesn't matter. The intimacy of the moment, the connection we share, overshadows any imperfections.

Lyric's hand comes to rest on my cheek, her fingers warm and soft. I respond in kind, my hand finding the small of her back, pulling her closer. The kiss is unhurried, a slow exploration. It's a kiss that speaks of comfort, love, and thousands of shared mornings to come.

When we finally pull back, her eyes are bright, and she's smiling in a way that makes my heart race.

"Coffee?" she suggests, her voice still a little drowsy.

"Yeah," I reply, grinning. "Coffee sounds good."

In this simple moment, I realize that love isn't about perfection. It's about sharing all the little things—the good and the bad—and still feeling like the luckiest person in the world.

***

After a shower, I walk downstairs and along the corridor to check on Lyric's dad, who is already in the infirmary.

"Mr. Fullerton," I greet, pushing open the door with a creak. He looks up, his eyes are sharp, and they track to me, searching, measuring. "Are you okay?"

Something flickers in his eyes, but he nods. "The girls are doing better, especially Mia. The things they endured." He shakes his head. "They should speak with a counselor."

"Too many secrets could come to light. Could you act as that for them for now?"

"I'm a plastic surgeon, not a psychologist."

I nod, not really knowing what else to say to this

man, so I change the subject. "Ahh, Lyric is making coffee. Would you like a cup?"

"Lyric?" He shakes his head again and moves closer to me. "I don't know what it is about your MC that has my girls so devoted to you, but know this, Highway, if you hurt Gwen, you'll have me to answer to."

With a nod, I say, "There'll be nothing for me to answer to you for. Lyric, like Lucy, fits in with us. She gets it." I step back into the hallway. "I hope you will too."

I keep walking to the kitchen, where Jet is talking to Lyric. Jet's smile is bright enough to chase away shadows. She's got the other women from the raid with her, and their chatter and smiles are letting me know they are not scared to be here.

Leaning against the doorway with my arms crossed, I watch the scene unfold. Jet catches my eye and winks, and I can't help but crack a grin. Yeah, we're doing something right here. And damn if it doesn't feel like a victory, at least for this moment.

"Highway," Jet calls, head tilted, inviting me in.

But I stay put like a sentinel at the gate.

"Everything good?" she asks.

"Good as gold," I reply, and it's true enough.

Lyric bounds toward me with a coffee cup in her hand. "For you."

"Thanks, babe." Her face lights up at my

endearment. "I think your dad could use a cup."

Mia smiles at me and shyly says, "I'll get it for him."

Jet rubs her arm, and all the women go back to the infirmary, leaving Lyric and me alone.

"Have you seen Creed?"

"Not yet. About to head in now." I hold up the cup. "Thanks for this."

"Come back when you're done, and I'll make you breakfast."

This all feels like it's meant to be, and I smile at her and head for the meeting room. When I open the door, Creed is sitting in his usual spot at the head of the table.

"Prez," I say by way of a greeting.

"Did you sleep?" he asks.

"Yeah, like a log."

"Good." He stands as I take my seat at the table. "The Ivanovs are coming to us. Lev wanted a sit-down and a conversation that can't be overheard by outside forces. I want all of you to stay sharp. No one is to leave the compound, and no one is to enter it today. Fingers will do sweeps looking for bugs, and I want you all to keep everyone happy. I know some of the women will want to leave, but you need to explain to them and their kids that, for today, they need to stay put." His lips turn down at the corners. "At least until after the meet. I don't need to tell you all how badly we need this to go in our favor." He takes a deep breath. "So, let's get to work keeping us and our loved ones safe."

***

The sun hangs low, a dying ember in the sky as they roll in—black sedans with tinted windows.

"Time to play nice with the big bad wolves," I mutter to myself, watching as Lev Ivanov steps out, flanked by six of his Russian shadows. They move with a predator's grace, all sharp suits and sharper eyes.

Ivanov is different. He blends like he's cut from the same cloth as this American wasteland we call home. No accent laces his words when he greets us with a nod, which is more calculation than courtesy.

"Highway," he says, his voice as smooth as a polished gun barrel. "Shall we?"

We file into the clubhouse, a room heavy with the scent of spilled beer and old smoke. It's our turf, our rules, but the Russians? They don't seem to care much for boundaries.

"Let's cut through the bullshit," Ivanov starts, taking a seat at our table without waiting for an invitation. Creed is already there as we all sit, a council of warlords in our own right. "You've done well clearing the path. Now it's time to push the Diablos out of Jacksonville."

His men mutter agreements in thick accents.

They're eager, hungry for the chaos to come. But Ivanov? His eyes are cold and calculating. This is chess, not checkers.

"Thanks to you, we have their supply routes. The rest will follow." Lev's hands gesture, painting pictures of a city free from rivals, a throne waiting for a new king. "It will be simple." Simple for him, maybe. A man who doesn't flinch at the thought of blood staining his manicured hands.

I lean back, arms folded, feeling the weight of every decision, every alliance forged in fire and necessity. The Russians might be our guests today, but tomorrow? Who knows which way the gun will be pointing?

Creed's chair scrapes the wooden floor, a harsh sound that cuts through the tense air. He leans in, tattoos on his forearms twisting with the movement.

"Lev," he says, his voice low and gritty. "The Diablos are dug in deep. Not just some rats we can smoke out."

Ivanov's lip curls up ever so slightly, a predator baring teeth to a lesser beast. "The Diablo Cartel is strong..." he concedes, tapping a finger on the table, "... but not invincible."

"I need to keep my club safe," Creed pushes, his eyes locked on the Russian. "That's the deal. We don't need another war on our doorstep."

"Da, of course," Lev replies. "Your safety is

paramount." But his eyes flicker with something else. Ambition, maybe? Or is it contempt?

"Timeline," I cut in. "We need specifics. Intel. When do we move?"

"Swiftly." Ivanov stands, commanding the space as if he owns it, which he damn well doesn't. "Two days. No more. Gather what you need. Prepare your men."

"Two days?" Creed's surprise mirrors my own, but there's no time for doubt. Our window is narrow, closing fast.

"Time is blood, gentlemen." Lev's smile doesn't reach his eyes. "And blood? It waits for no one."

Lev Ivanov places his hands on the back of his chair, the ghost of a smirk playing on his lips. I watch him, trying to read between the lines.

"Diablos..." he begins, rolling the word off his tongue like it's personal, "... they're no street gang. They've got reach. Power." He pauses, eyeing each of us in turn. "But they bleed like the rest. A predator knows the strength of its prey."

"Prey implies you're going to eat them alive," Creed says.

"Exactly," Lev agrees, his confidence a palpable force in the room.

"Your plan?" I prod because we're all thinking it. If Lev's so sure, he's got to have an ace up his sleeve.

"Simple," Lev holds his arms wide as if embracing the challenge. "We strike at their heart...

Camilla and her father, Mateo. Without them, the Diablos crumble."

"Her brother, Gabriel?" I throw in, skeptical. There's always a wild card, and blood ties run deep.

Lev laughs, sharp and cold. "The brother? Please. He doesn't have the balls to lead, let alone fill his sister's shoes." His gaze is steely, confident. "Another will rise, but by then, they'll be limping. Market share gone, their reputation in tatters."

"Easy pickings for you," I conclude, the plan unfolding in my mind. It's bold and brash, but it just might work.

"Da," Lev confirms, the hint of a Russian lilt coloring the word. "They won't even see us coming until it's too late."

I exchange a look with Creed. This is big. Dangerous. But if we pull it off, we could change the game for good.

Creed stands, and I notice he's not wearing the sling. He holds out his hand to Lev, and they shake. For us and our world, this is all the guarantee we need—a simple handshake to seal the deal.

"A deal between the Royal Bastards and the Ivanovs," Creed says as they shake.

"Indeed. We'll let you know how it plays out."

With that, the Russians file out, the low rumble of their engines a fading growl outside.

I turn to Creed, his voice is low. "Keep your eyes on them. Can't trust a damn word they say."

"Will do," I grunt, already at the door.

I scan the room, the tension still hanging in the air. But it's her I'm looking for—Lyric. She's the one who's got me hooked bad. I find her at the edge of the crowd, her hair cascading down her back. Our eyes lock, and something electric zips through me, fierce and protective.

"Lyric," I call across the room, my tone more urgent than I intended. She pushes through the others, her movements graceful, even in the thick of leather and denim.

"Highway?" Her voice is steady, but her eyes search mine.

We move outside, away from prying eyes and ears.

"Stay close," I say, gripping her shoulders just enough to feel the warmth of her skin. "This play with the Ivanovs, it's gonna get dirty. I need you safe."

She doesn't flinch from my touch. Instead, she leans in slightly. "I can handle a bit of dirt."

"Lyric..." I start, but she places a finger over my lips, silencing me.

"Trust me," she whispers. "I'm not going anywhere, and the women from the other MC, they're keen to meet the club women here." She looks over her shoulder and waves at Jet. "Go do what you need to do, and I'll be here with them."

As I watch her go, she's suddenly surrounded by

new faces, women from a fallen MC, lost and looking for a foothold. Lyric stands among them, her voice rising above the rest as she introduces them to our clubhouse women. They're hesitant, glancing around like cornered animals, but Lyric is there, the bridge between two worlds. A smile plays on my lips—she's a natural, bringing light into the darkest corners.

"Hey, look at you..." I say when she catches my eye again, "... playing the MC diplomat."

"Someone's got to," she shoots back with a grin that hits me square in the chest.

"Come here," I beckon her over, knowing full well I should be talking strategy with Reaper or Winchester as we keep an eye on the Russians. But hell, she's under my skin now, and I'm not about to pretend otherwise.

As she steps closer, the club buzzing around us, I lean in, my words for her only. "Once this is over, we're taking a ride, you and I. Just the open road and no looking back."

"Promise?" She tilts her head.

"Cross my heart," I answer, sealing it with the faintest touch to her cheek.

"Good." She smiles and, with a last lingering look, turns back to the women.

My gut twists. This thing with the Diablos, it's a high-stakes game. And I'll be damned if I let it take down what's slowly becoming mine.

Walking into our meeting room, Creed and Reaper are leaning over the table, its surface scarred from past brawls.

"Those women…" Creed says as he looks out at them, "… we need some assurances from them."

Reaper nods, his eyes hooded. "Yeah. They can't stay here forever. And we can't let them leave until we know where they stand."

Creed is quiet for a beat too long. Then he pushes off the table, his leather jacket creaking. "I'll handle it."

He strides toward them. "Ladies, could you please come with me to the infirmary?" He doesn't wait for an answer but strides through the clubhouse, shoulders set like he's marching into war.. The women file in one by one, wary gazes meeting his square-on.

"Listen up," Creed's voice slices through the silence. "Once we settle the score with the Diablos, you're free to go. But answer me this…" His gaze locks on each one. "Any of you even think about running to the cops—"

He doesn't get to finish before Jet speaks, her spine straightening. "We owe you our lives," she says. "There's nothing we've seen, nothing worth talking about."

The others follow suit, a sea of nodding heads.

Mia is softer, almost shy. "Is it… *okay*, if I stick

around?" Her voice barely makes it across the room.

Creed's face cracks just a fraction, happiness flickering in his cold eyes. Then it's gone. "Fine," he grunts. "But play by our rules."

"Understood," she whispers, relief flooding her features.

I watch from the doorway, my chest tight.

This life, these choices, there's no going back now.

Chapter 17

Lyric

Once the meeting with the Russians was over, Reaper announced we were allowed to leave the compound if we wanted. Highway left not long after the Russians, so I decided to go home and collect a few more things.

The door to my home swings open with a groan, the familiar creak giving me a false sense of security. Which soon gives way to apprehension.

Everything is wrong.

"Son of a bitch," I mutter, stepping inside.

The place is trashed. Cushions are slashed, drawers are emptied, and pictures are smashed on the floor. Memories are spilled out all over the carpet This was my sanctuary, and now it's a war zone.

"Dammit." My voice echoes through the

wreckage. "Is anyone here? I've called the police." No answer. Just the sound of my shoes crunching over shattered glass.

I move deeper, every room telling the same violent story. Whoever did this was looking for something or sending a message.

Who would do this?

Diablos? Russians? Revenge or a warning?

But who? Why now? The questions claw at my mind as I sift through the debris.

My cell phone rings, and I jump at the noise. Clutching my chest, I pull it out of my back pocket.

"Hello?"

"Where are you?" Highway asks.

"I went home to get a few things." My voice is a little too high.

"What's wrong?"

"Someone broke in, and they've smashed everything."

"Stay there, lock the doors. I'll come as soon as I can. I'm not far away."

I nod, even though he can't see it. "I'm not scared."

"You should be," he says, half-joking. But we both know it's true. "Lock yourself in the bathroom until I get there. Do not open the door for anyone but me. Understood?"

"Will do."

I end the call and walk to my bedroom, feeling a

knot of anxiety tightening in my stomach. The sight that greets me is one of utter chaos. The mattress has been violently slashed, its stuffing spilling out like entrails. My personal belongings are scattered haphazardly across the floor, creating a landscape of disarray and violation.

I crouch down and reach under the bed, feeling for the familiar coolness of the metal suitcase I keep there. My fingers close around it, and I pull it out. Quickly, I start gathering a few clothes and personal items, shoving them into the suitcase with hurried, jerky movements.

Suddenly, the sound of something crashing to the floor in another room pierces the silence, sending a jolt of fear through me. With my heart pounding, I abandon the suitcase and dash into the bathroom, slamming the door shut behind me. I lock it with trembling hands and press my back against it, breathing heavily as I try to calm my racing thoughts.

My heart hammers against my chest like it's trying to break free. Every creak and whisper of movement beyond the bathroom door sends a fresh wave of ice coursing through my veins. I'm crouched behind the shower curtain, barely breathing, my eyes fixed on the sliver of light under the door. It feels like I've been in here for hours.

"Lyric!" His voice, rough and urgent, cuts through the suffocating silence.

Highway.

"Here! I'm in here!" My voice is a strangled whisper, muscles tensed for flight.

The door bursts open, and there he stands, his presence filling the space with raw power and an undercurrent of danger.

"Jesus, Lyric." Relief colors his tone as he strides in. His eyes scan me from head to toe, assessing, always protecting. "You okay?"

"Scared out of my mind," I admit, pushing past the fear to stand. He wraps an arm around me, pulling me close for a moment before we step back into the chaos.

The living room is a disaster, a storm of broken memories and violated spaces—glass glittering like diamonds scattered across the floor and drawers upended, their contents strewn throughout my home.

"Who would do this?" Anger laces my words with venom.

My gaze darts around, searching for answers in the wreckage.

"Could be anyone. Past grudges or new threats." Highway's eyes are hard, scanning the destruction with tactical precision. He moves through the room, boots crunching on debris, touching nothing but seeing everything.

"Someone's sending a message," I say, my mind racing as I try to piece together the puzzle. The air feels heavy with menace, the silence louder than any scream.

Highway's jaw clenches. "Maybe, but they just signed up for a war."

We stand amidst the remnants of a life interrupted, our hearts beating to the rhythm of impending retribution.

"How could you be so stupid to put yourself in danger? What were you thinking?"

Surprised at his outburst, I turn to face him. "Reaper said we could leave the compound, and I wanted a few more clothes. Honestly, I

didn't think it would be a problem."

Highway throws his arm out in an arc and shakes his head. "That's the problem, Lyric, you don't think. If whoever did this was still here, you could have been hurt. And..." He takes a deep breath and lowers his voice. "I'm not sure I could deal with that."

Moving closer to him, I put an arm around his waist. "You like me," I tease. His mouth goes into a hard line. "I'm so sorry. I won't do it again."

He quirks an eyebrow up at me and kisses me lightly. "Something tells me you will."

With a shrug, I step away from him. "I'll try my best."

Bending down, I turn over a picture frame, and my fingers stumble upon a jagged edge, an anomaly in the sea of debris. A photograph. I snatch it up, a

Polaroid from a time when innocence wasn't a memory. My breath catches. It's Lucy, her smile frozen in a happier yesterday, but where there should be two, there's only one. The other half is torn away.

"Highway, look at this."

He bends down and holds out a hand. "What is it?"

"An old picture of Lucy and Dom." The name tastes like bile. "But someone ripped him out."

"Dom?" Highway's brow furrows, a storm brewing in his eyes. "The Loco's Dom?"

"Exactly." My heart hammers.

A message? A threat?

"Shit." He curses under his breath. "Pack a bag, Lyric. We're heading to the clubhouse."

No arguments there. I walk back into my bedroom and shove clothes into my discarded suitcase with trembling hands.

Outside, the night's cool embrace does nothing to calm my nerves. Highway mounts his Harley. I place my suitcase on the truck's seat, taking one last look at the home, now scarred by violence.

"Let's go. I'll follow you."

Not needing to be told twice, I start the engine and speed through the streets, with the clubhouse as our destination.

It promises safety. Maybe answers.

When I pull into the compound, I park the truck

in its usual spot. Highway pulls alongside me, and I wind down the window.

"Find your dad and Lucy. I'll get Reaper."

"Got it." My head is on a swivel as I push through the doors.

Lucy is sitting at a table with Dad. They're talking, and he's smiling at her. It feels like forever since I've seen him smile. Dad is dressed in jeans and a T-shirt. Not his usual clothes, but he blends in better in the clubhouse. He sees me and waves.

"I need to speak to you both outside."

They follow without question, and I lead them toward the bonfire burning at the back of the clubhouse. Only a handful of people are near it, and when Reaper appears, they leave us alone.

"What's going on?" asks Reaper.

"Someone's broken into our home, Dad," I start, the torn Polaroid clenched in my fist like a verdict. "It could have something to do with this."

"Might be the Locos," Highway adds.

I glance at him, then back at Lucy, and hold out the photograph. "I had this in my bedroom. It was an old photo of you and Dom."

Lucy takes the torn image and says, "Why would you have a picture of me and Dom?"

"I took it a long time ago. And it wasn't kept because of Dom but you. When you disappeared from us, I kept lots of your stuff. I missed you," I confess.

Lucy's lips turn down, and she looks upset.

"Too close," Reaper growls, the bonfire reflecting in his eyes.

The fire crackles and pops, sending a shower of sparks and embers into the night sky. The warm glow flickers shadows across his face.

I draw in a sharp breath, the torn Polaroid gripped tight in Lucy's hand.

Reaper's hand clenches into a fist, his knuckles white as bone. "Damn Locos," he spits out, fury radiating off him like exhaust heat.

Lucy edges closer to him, her eyes wide and fearful. "I thought we were done with them."

"Hey," Reaper's voice softens as he cradles her face, his thumb brushing her cheek. "Me too. I'll fix this."

"How?" Dad asks.

"We'll figure it out. If this is the Locos or someone close to them, we will find them," Reaper vows.

"Nothing will touch either of you," Highway declares, and damn if I don't believe every word.

"Good." I nod, and Lucy throws the torn photograph into the fire.

"I'll have Fingers work his magic and see if there are any loose ends with the Locos. Until we know who it is, you should all stay close to the clubhouse," advises Reaper.

Dad puts a hand on Lucy's shoulder. "So long as

my girls are here, I'm happy to stay, but I need to be getting back to work."

Reaper nods. "We'll work it out. It could be a simple robbery."

Highway frowns. "It didn't look like anything was missing."

"Maybe it was kids messing about," I offer.

Reaper and Highway exchange a glance.

"Yeah, could be," replies Reaper, but he doesn't sound confident.

Dad yawns. "I've got a big day tomorrow. I'm hitting the hay."

"Come on," Highway growls, a command that rumbles through me.

I nod, the lingering heat from the bonfire at our backs as we walk back through the clubhouse. We go up to our room, and he shuts the door, sealing us away from the chaos of the outside world.

He doesn't speak, but his eyes say everything. It's just us now, Highway and me.

"Safe," I murmur against his chest, the word muffled by the fabric of his cut.

"Yeah."

His hands are on me then, urgent and demanding, peeling away layers of clothing. I meet him with equal passion, pulling at buckles and zippers.

"Lyric," he breathes out as his lips crash against mine in a heated collision.

"Highway," I gasp, giving as good as I get.

Our movements are frantic, a dance of need and assurance.

He hoists me up, and I wrap around him, a tangle of limbs. The bed is there, a soft landing in a hard world, but we barely notice, too caught up in the urgency of now.

"Show me," I dare between kisses, challenging the protector in him, the beast always ready to defend and claim.

"Mine." He growls.

The hard planes of his body crush against the soft curves of mine.

"Yours," I affirm, surrendering to the waves of passion and power that crash over us.

His eyes meet mine, and the world around us blurs into insignificance. I can feel my heart pounding, the anticipation building like a tidal wave. He crushes me against his skin, the electric intensity between us seems almost painful. My breath catches in my throat as his hand gently cradles my cheek, his touch sending shivers down my spine.

Highway's lips hover over mine, and I feel the warmth of his breath mingling with my own.

A surge of emotion crashes over me as his mouth moves against mine, soft yet insistent. His kiss is tender and fervent, a perfect blend of desire and affection. My hands find their way to his shoulders, pulling him closer, wanting to melt into him completely. His fingers tangle in my hair, and I revel in the sensation, every nerve ending alive.

We lose ourselves in the kiss, a dance of lips and tongues that leaves me breathless and wanting more. It's a kiss that speaks volumes, conveying a depth of feeling words could never capture. When we finally pull apart, our foreheads resting against each other, I open my eyes to see the same passion reflected in his. The world slowly comes back into focus, but I'm forever changed, marked by the intensity of our connection.

Highway grins and claims my lips once more, our tongues exploring and tasting each other with hunger and desperation. The essence of him, a mixture of spice and heat, ignites my senses and urges me to give more. My skin is alive with sensation, every touch sending sparks of electricity through me, igniting a fire that can only be quenched by more of him. My hands roam freely, exploring every inch of skin, claiming and possessing with each caress. I can see the sweat glistening on Highway's tattooed skin, the lines of his muscles taut with exertion. Our bodies are pressed tightly together, my skin tingling with the friction of our movements. His grip on me is strong, protective, and possessive as if he never wants to let me go.

Highway's cock is poised at my entrance, and he

slowly eases himself inside me. A gasp escapes me as he rocks back, only to push his way back in. My body is on fire. Highway puts a hand on either side of my head, and I wrap my legs around his waist. He bucks into me again and again, hitting me just right.

"Harder," I plead.

Highway grins and increases his speed, but it's not enough. I plant my foot on the bed, and he lets me flip us, and I ride his cock. His hands go to my hips, and he moves me faster as though he is also on the precipice. His teeth are bared, and his hair is a slick mess as we move in unison, chasing our release.

Highway's mouth falls open, his eyes closed, and his fingernails bite into my hips, pushing me over the edge. A moan escapes me as I ride him, my whole body pulsing with the orgasm that washes through me.

"Fuuck!" His curse signaling he has also found his release.

With a hand on his chest, I keep moving until every last wave of passion is extinguished. Highway's eyes open, and he smiles.

"You're so fucking beautiful." He reaches up and cups one of my breasts, his calloused thumb brushing over my nipple. "Mine."

"Yours."

Highway knifes up and kisses me, a low growl

emanating from him while his hands hold me close.

I feel cherished and, dare I say it, loved.

***

The vibration against the bar's sticky surface jars me. A text from an unknown number glares up from my phone.

Unknown*: Warehouse off route 22. Midnight. Come alone.*

"Damn," I mutter, thumbing over the keys.

No name. No explanation. Just a command wrapped in mystery and the hint of danger. My gut twists into knots, but this could be a story.

"Meet who?" I whisper to myself.

Curiosity claws at me. It could be a trap, a setup, a deadly game with me as the pawn. But it could also be information. I scan the clubhouse, and no one is paying me much attention. Highway is in a meeting with the MC's senior members, and the door to their meeting room is shut.

"Lyric, you're a damned fool," I chide, shoving the phone into my jacket's pocket.

"Going somewhere?" asks a voice behind me.

Turning, it's Justice. "Maybe I am," I shoot back with a grin.

Justices shakes his head, but his eyes are already on Jet, who has emerged from the infirmary. Seeing he's distracted, I stride toward the door. This could be information on the break-in or, better yet, a story to sell to the highest bidder.

As I push through the door, the night air hits me like a slap—cold and crisp, filled with the scent of impending rain. I climb into Winchester's truck, and the metal beast rumbles to life with the turning of the key. According to Google, it shouldn't take me more than twenty minutes to reach my destination, leaving me at least five minutes before the allotted time.

***

The rusted chain on the warehouse door screeches a protest as I nudge it open, and my boots echo in the cavernous space. The smell of decay hits me hard. I venture farther in and see a dead rat on the concrete floor, while dim lights flicker overhead, casting long, dancing shadows.

"Hello?" My voice seems to bounce off the walls, coming back to me twisted and unfamiliar.

A figure steps out of the darkness, heels clicking sharply, deliberate and slow. She stands there, bathed in the sickly yellow glow from a single hanging bulb, her features obscured.

"Been waiting long?" I ask, my hand inching

toward the knife hidden inside my jacket at the back.

"Long enough," she replies.

Her silhouette moves closer, the light revealing the sharp angles of her face, eyes glinting with something feral.

"Who are you?" I keep my tone even and calm, but inside, my pulse hammers.

"Someone with answers." Her lips curve, not quite a smile.

"Answers to what?" I shift from foot to foot.

"Questions you haven't even thought to ask." She takes a step. I frown at her, and she says, "We'll get there, Lyric. We'll get there soon enough."

The woman leans in, close enough that I can see the color of her eyes and her blown pupils. She's on something.

"I got dirt on the Diablos," she whispers through gritted teeth. "It's the kind that could burn it all down."

I frown, instinctively taking a half step back. "And you just had to share this with me?" My voice is steady, but inside, my thoughts race.

"Damn straight." She spits the words out like they burn her tongue. "But it ain't charity, girl. This is business."

"Business? So why not take this up with our prez? Why the cloak and dagger with me?"

She smirks, an ugly twist of her lips. "Because,

sweetheart, sometimes it's the one who doesn't bark who bites the hardest."

"If you think cozying up to me will get you anywhere—"

"Cozy ain't in my vocabulary," she cuts in. "But leverage is. And right now, you're it."

The stale air in the warehouse grows thick with tension.

The woman's face contorts, a snarl pulling at her lips. "You think you're smart, don't ya?" Her voice is a low growl.

I hold my ground though every instinct screams to bolt. "Smart enough not to trust easily," I shoot back, gripping the knife behind me tighter.

"Too smart," she spits, her eyes narrowing into slits. "You're playing a dangerous game." A bitter chuckle escapes her as she takes another menacing step forward. "I was Venom's Ol' Lady, girl. President of the Crimson Wheelers."

Chills race down my spine, and I inch away, my boots scraping against the concrete.

Jesus Christ! I'm in deep, way over my head.

"Venom..." I hiss under my breath.

"Got it in one," she sneers, prowling closer like a predator circling its prey.

I swallow hard, retreating until my back meets cold metal. Nowhere left to run.

Movement flickers in the periphery, a shadow detaching from darkness. Highway. My pulse spikes, a cocktail of fear and relief flooding my veins. Reaper slinks beside him, ghost-like. They move with lethal grace, unnoticed by the woman whose focus is locked on me.

Backup has arrived, but the danger isn't over. Not by a long shot.

"Tell me," I demand, sidestepping away from her. "Why come after me?"

She paces like a caged animal. "Followed Highway, didn't I? To your cozy little home." Her lips curl back, exposing yellowed, rotting teeth. "Tore it apart, looking for something, anything, to hit the Bastards where it hurts."

My heart pounds. This woman invaded my home.

A cold laugh tumbles from her, echoing in the warehouse. "Killing you?" She shakes her head, a twisted amusement in her eyes. "Not as sweet as taking down one of them. One of them Bastards, but it'll do."

Her confession hangs heavy in the air. My gaze flickers to the shadows to where Highway and Reaper stay hidden.

Electric silence crackles between us. I swallow hard, every muscle taut, ready to spring, to flee. But where? This is a trap, and I walked straight into it.

"Then come on," I taunt, my voice low, eyes locked on hers. "Do what you came for."

She lurches—a sudden blur of motion, all rage

and recklessness. My breath hitches, and adrenaline surges as the distance closes between us.

In that heartbeat, the shadow becomes a savior. Highway steps out. A ghost turned guardian. His presence, a silent promise—I am not alone in this dance with death.

"Lyric, watch out!" His voice shatters the tension.

The woman's hand whips forward, steel glinting in the dim light, a knife aimed with deadly precision. Time slows, and my body coils, ready to twist away.

"Highway…" A whisper, a prayer, as metal approaches.

Her arm descends, fury etched into every line of her being, the knife plunging down.

Darkness swallows my scream, and the world freezes.

Chapter 18

Highway

I'm a heartbeat away from being too late. Adrenaline surges as my boots pound the concrete, closing the distance to Lyric. The woman's arm is a coiled viper, the blade glinting with deadly intent.

Please, God, no.

"Lyric!" My voice rips through the tension.

Her scream pierces the chaos, slicing through me. But as I surge forward, fueled by raw panic and something fiercer—protectiveness—the distance between us shrinks to nothing. My hand lashes out, fingers wrapping around the attacker's wrist with an iron grip.

I twist hard, the motion as natural as breathing, born of brawls and battles fought in the name of brotherhood. Bones snap, a sound like dry wood splintering in a campfire. The blade clatters to the concrete.

The woman's scream morphs into one of pain, high and ragged. Her face contorts, eyes wild with shock and agony. She crumples, but I don't ease up until I'm sure she's no longer a threat to Lyric.

"Stay down," I growl, the command rumbling deep within my chest.

My heart still races, thumping against my ribcage like it's trying to break free. I lock eyes with Lyric, whose gaze swims with unshed tears and relief. But we're not done here—not by a long shot.

Reaper is there in a flash, his large frame a barricade between Lyric and the crumpled woman. He yanks her back by her jacket's collar like he's pulling a sack of trash from the curb. And me? I'm shaking, vibrating with a fury that's got nowhere to go now but out.

"Dammit, Lyric!" My voice is a snarl, a beast unleashed. "You could've been killed! What the hell were you thinking, not telling anyone where you were headed?"

My hands are fists at my sides, every muscle coiled tight. It's a miracle I had that tracker on her phone, a lifeline she didn't even know she had.

Her eyes are wide, shock giving way to the realization of what just went down. She starts to speak, her voice small against the roar in my ears, "Highway, I—"

"Save it," I bite out, cutting her off. There's no room for excuses. Not now. Not when she was a hair's breadth away from a blade ending everything.

Reaper's chuckle cuts through my rage, but it's hollow, lacking any real mirth. "Girl, you're more trouble than your sister ever was," he says, shaking his head. His hand still grips the woman, keeping her at bay. "But damn if I don't have a soft spot for Lucy. Means you're family, like it or not."

Lyric's trying to stitch herself back together, an apology trembling on her lips. But Reaper isn't done. The laughter drains from his face, leaving it cold as a slab in the morgue. His next words are a low growl meant for her and her alone.

"Don't be so reckless, Lyric. Never, ever dare to be so stupid as to go it alone. That's not what Bastards do! If you want to be part of us then act like it!"

The air is electric with his warning, his protectiveness something fierce and unyielding. For a moment, nobody moves. We're all caught in the gravity of his words, the unspoken consequences hanging heavy between us.

Reaper's grip is iron as he hauls the woman away, her curses trailing like exhaust fumes. I watch them go, tension coiling in my gut.

Lyric is beside me, quivering slightly. She's been through hell, but she's still standing, tough as they come. Her eyes catch mine, full of remorse.

"Highway, I'm so sorry—"

"Stop talking." My voice is gravelly, raw with anger and fear tangled together. "You think sorry is gonna cut it?"

She flinches, and I hate myself for it, but the rage is a living thing inside me. "I love you." The words are harsh, clipped with the effort it takes to keep from shaking her. "But if you pull a stunt like this again…" My hand balls into a fist. "I swear, Lyric, you won't sit down for a week."

Her breath catches, eyes wide and fixed on me. There's fear there, yes, but underneath it, something that looks like wonder.

The words hang in the air, raw and jagged. I can see them hitting her, slicing through the panic and fear. Her lips part, tears brimming in those wide, haunted eyes.

"Highway," she whispers, voice trembling. "I love you too." It's a confession ripped from somewhere deep, a truth laid bare between us.

My heart hammers against my ribs, a drumbeat of war and want. This woman, my Lyric, brave and reckless, has me by the soul. I step forward, closing the gap, my hands finding her face.

"Lyric," I growl, every emotion I've got bleeding into her name.

Our lips crash together, electric and desperate. I kiss her like I'm claiming her, branding her as mine with every sweep of my tongue. She meets me with fire and a need that echoes my own, her arms winding around my neck.

I'm all hard lines and rough edges, and she's soft curves and fierce spirit. My kiss tells her everything—my anger, my fear, and my love. It's all there in the push and pull, the give and take.

"You belong to me," I murmur against her lips, a promise, a vow.

"Yes," she breathes back, and it's all the surrender I need.

***

We arrive back at the clubhouse, Lyric's hand clutched in mine, trembling but alive. The infirmary door swings open with a thud that echoes my racing pulse. There, Justice is working on the woman, wrapping her arm in a sling, his face as hard as the steel of his tools.

"Sit tight," he orders.

I scan the room, taking in the sterile smell of antiseptics and the sight of Reaper leaning against a wall. His eyes are locked on the woman.

"Talk," Reaper demands, and I can feel the threat in his voice vibrating in my chest.

She shrugs, nonchalant even with her arm busted. "Tore lots of things," she says casually as if discussing the weather.

"Coincidence, my ass," Reaper snaps, stepping closer. He's a predator cornering his prey. "The photo. Why'd you take the other half?"

Her head shakes, and she frowns. "Didn't take nothing."

Reaper's stance tightens, coiling like a spring. "Bullshit," he spits out.

Justice finishes securing the sling and steps back. It's meant to make her feel safe and think she'll be released, but it's all an act. Her eyes dart around the room, perhaps sensing the deceit, searching for an escape that doesn't exist.

A silent moment passes. "Better start making sense," Reaper warns, his voice low and dangerous.

I squeeze Lyric's hand, a silent reminder that I'm here and with her.

Lyric's fingers entwine with mine. "The other half..." Lyric says, her voice hesitant, "... it might be back at the house. Under all that mess... we didn't sift through all of it. I found it ripped in two and assumed..."

Reaper's heavy sigh cuts through the tension, his shoulders relaxing ever so slightly—a stark contrast to the coiled intensity from moments ago. "So, it ain't the Locos then," he concludes, almost to himself but loud enough for us to catch. The relief in his voice doesn't quite mask the underlying frustration. "Just a crazy woman causing havoc."

Lyric flinches beside me, and I pull her closer,

wrapping an arm around her shoulder. Reaper's eyes meet mine, a silent nod passing between us. We've been through worse scrapes, but every time danger nips at our heels, it leaves a mark. This time, it's a reminder that even in our world, sometimes the chaos is just madness, not the enemy trying to destroy us.

The infirmary door squeaks open, a slice of light slicing the dimness. Jet's unmistakable silhouette fills the gap. She takes one step in, two, then freezes like she's hit an invisible wall.

"Foxy," she breathes out, her voice barely a whisper but loaded with a thousand unspoken words. Her eyes lock onto the woman we've been grappling with, and I see something flicker across her face—fear, recognition, disgust? Hard to tell.

Jet backs out, retreating into the shadows as if she's seen a ghost.

Justice, who's been doing his best to bandage up Foxy's broken arm, shoots a look at the woman. "What'd you do to Jet?" he asks, his voice low and dangerous.

Foxy, sitting on the edge of a cot, her good arm cradling the sling, shrugs. There's no remorse there, no fear either. It's like she's discussing the weather, not the potential fallout of her actions.

"Those other chicks?" Foxy says, a sneer curling her lip. "They ain't like me. They were there for one thing only." She spits the next words out like they're poison. "Lying on their backs. Servicing the Crimson Wheelers." She laughs, and it's a sharp, ugly sound. "Nothing but whores."

I clench my fists, hands are balled up in tension while anger builds. This woman, this... Foxy, she's got a lot of nerve. But I've got to stay cool, keep my head.

"Watch your mouth," Justice warns, the threat clear in his tone.

Foxy smirks like she's untouchable and doesn't care what comes next.

Reaper's gaze locks onto Foxy, ice-cold and merciless. The air in the infirmary thickens with tension, and I can damn near taste the danger on my tongue.

"Time to go," Reaper says, his voice flat as a dead engine.

He doesn't need to raise his voice. Doesn't have to. His presence alone commands the room. Justice nods, stepping forward, his large frame blocking the light as he moves toward Foxy.

"Move," Justice grunts, no hint of a question in his tone.

Foxy stands, her smirk finally wiped off her face. She knows better than to argue. They all do when Reaper's got that look in his eyes—the one that spells out trouble with a capital T.

They march her out, Reaper leading the way, Justice at the rear, like she's some kind of prisoner.

Which, hell, maybe she is. Maybe she has always been. The clubhouse door swings shut with a sound that echoes like a final verdict.

"Where are they taking her?" Jet asks behind me.

"Doesn't matter," I reply, keeping my voice low. "It's club business."

But my gut twists, uneasy.

The night's dark, and it's hungry. Hungry for secrets, sins, and whatever Reaper's got planned.

I watch through the window. They are only silhouettes now, three shadows swallowed by the night. No words. No goodbyes. Just the quiet crunch of gravel under heavy boots.

Then, they disappear around the corner of the clubhouse, and it's like they were never here—like Foxy was never there.

"Think they'll..." Jet's words trail off, not finishing her thought. Not out loud.

"Maybe," I say. "Or maybe they'll just teach her a lesson she won't forget."

We all know Reaper's capable of both. And then some.

The night is silent and so am I, but the clubhouse carries on. Laughter spills from the bar, the jukebox kicks back to life, and somewhere, a bottle shatters.

"Let's get a drink," I tell the curious Jet, clapping her on the shoulder and steering her away from the window. "Whatever happens, happens. It's Reaper's call."

But my eyes linger on that corner where darkness swallowed them whole. And I can't help but wonder if Foxy's about to become just another ghost story we tell around the fire.

Chapter 19

Highway

The rumble of motorcycle engines soothes me as we cruise down the highway. I'm at the tail end, eyes peeled for trouble because that's what road captains do. Watch. Protect. Ride.

Ahead, Creed's bike slows. We must be pulling over. We are near the Old Dixie Highway, so I throttle down, feeling the drag, and the boys follow suit.

"Circle up," Creed grunts, his voice rough like gravel tossed in a metal bucket. He's off his Harley, his boots kicking up dust.

I kill my engine. The sudden quiet is a stark contrast to the relentless thrum of the ride.

Creed's stance is all wrong. He's favoring his left side, shoulder dipped low. The wound in his shoulder must be giving him some pain.

"Russians say we wait here," Creed says through gritted teeth. His hand hovers over his shoulder. "They got a *present* for us."

"Present, huh?" Reaper snorts, but there's an edge to his voice.

A present from the Russians could be anything from a crate of AKs to a one-way ticket to a shallow grave.

"Any idea what kind of gift?" I ask.

"Guess we'll find out." Creed's eyes are steel, cold, and hard. He's expecting a delivery all right, just not the usual kind.

We settle in, engines cooling, the tension rising like heat from the blacktop.

Creed fishes out a couple of painkillers from his pocket, tilts his head back, and swallows them dry.

"Good to go?" I call over to him.

He nods, a tight jerk of his chin. "Hate this," he grunts. "Being out here, away from home turf... dealing with Ivanov's goons." His eyes darken, haunted. "But because the Diablos screwed us, we have no choice."

I watch Creed, the man who took a bullet and still rides like he owns the road. I've never seen him steer us wrong. Not once. He's got a code, and it's kept us alive. But things have changed since Devil entered his life. She's softened his edges without dulling his blade. Made him more human. And the club is all the better for it—tighter and stronger.

Yeah, we're in deep with the Russians now, but if there's a way through this mess, Creed will find it. He always does.

The rumble of an engine in the distance snags my attention. Dust plumes up from the Old Dixie Highway like a bad omen. I squint against the glare of the afternoon sun. Reaper catches the sound, too, his head tilting slightly.

"Truck's coming," he says, voice steady.

"Here?" Creed grunts, disbelief lacing his tone. "They normally stick to the main highway."

"Could be anyone." Reaper's hand hovers near his sidearm, eyes locked on the approaching vehicle. "Could be trouble."

"Or could be just what we're expecting," I toss in, but I'm scanning the stretch of road, wary. There aren't many reasons for a truck to roll through here. It could be lost.

Winchester's voice cuts through the tension. "Might wanna play it safe. Justice and I can take to the trees... keep an eye out."

Creed looks at him, a ghost of a smirk twisting his lips despite the pain etched in his face. "It's a damn truck, Winchester, not a goddamn ambush."

"Right," Winchester drawls, but the look he shoots me says he isn't convinced. "But you know how I love nature."

"Me too," Justice says.

"Fine," Creed concedes. "Go be one with the

wilderness, boys."

Justice's nod is quick, a silent agreement. He reaches into his saddlebags with practiced ease, pulling out the Glock. It gleams for just a split second before he tucks it away, hidden but ready. He doesn't say a word as he melts into the trees, blending into the scenery. Winchester follows suit, just another whisper in the wind, vanishing without a trace.

"Always the cautious one." Creed chuckles, shaking his head.

"Better safe than sorry," Reaper adds, though his eyes never stray from the dust cloud that's heralding the truck's arrival.

"Let's see what this *present* is all about, then," Creed says, flexing his injured shoulder with a wince.

"Ready for whatever's coming," I reply, my hand resting on the grip of my piece. The comfort of cold metal under my fingers steadies me.

"Let's hope it's just a delivery," Reaper mutters.

But we're all thinking the same thing—in our world, nothing is ever just anything.

The rumble of the truck grows louder, its engine growling like some caged beast finally set free. Something about this whole setup feels off.

The truck rolls to a stop, and the driver's door swings open with a creak. A mountain of a man steps out, boots thudding on the asphalt. His frame is bulky, muscles straining under the fabric of his shirt as if the cotton is a second skin.

"Present," he grunts, his accent thick, the syllables rough around the edges. He thrusts the keys toward Creed, who takes them without flinching. "For you."

"Who are you?" Reaper demands, voice like gravel.

"Boris," the man says, tapping his chest with a meaty finger. His eyes dart between us, sizing us up as friends or foes.

Creed pockets the keys, his face unreadable. "What kind of present?"

"Good present." Boris' attempt at reassurance comes across more like a warning.

I take a step forward, my instincts screaming.

What if this goes south?

What if it's a trap?

But I push those thoughts down and lock them away. No room for doubt now.

"Let's see it then," Creed's voice is steady.

Boris strides to the back of the truck, a hulking mass of confidence. The grin plastered on his face says we are either about to strike gold or walk into a damn ambush. I follow closely behind Creed and Reaper, my gut tight with anticipation.

"Come, come," Boris calls out, waving us on like we're old pals at a reunion rather than potential rivals or targets.

"Showtime," Reaper mutters, and there's that flicker in his eyes, the one that speaks of danger and excitement all wrapped up in one deadly package.

The truck doors fly open with a metallic crash that echoes off the trees. They stand wide like the gates to some forbidden armory. Inside, it's a goddammed arsenal. Row upon row of sleek, deadly firearms gleam under the Florida sun. My pulse kicks up a notch. This isn't just hardware—it's a statement.

"Fuck," Creed exhales, long and slow, a whistle cutting through the still air.

"Present from Camilla Sanchez." Boris beams. His eyes crinkle at the corners, and there's this glint of triumph in them.

"Jesus," Reaper says, his voice low and thoughtful. He's eyeing a rocket launcher like it's Christmas morning, and he's ten years old again.

"Sanchez?" Creed's brow creases into a frown, his voice rough like gravel. "How?"

Boris' smile doesn't falter as he runs a finger across his thick neck—a universal gesture that needs no translation. The Russian's eyes glint with dark humor, and there's a hint of finality in the move that sends a shiver down my spine.

Gifts like these come with strings. But right now, they look a lot like opportunity. And we're in no position to turn down any advantage.

"Very generous," Boris agrees, nodding

enthusiastically. There's an eagerness in his stance, like he's waiting for applause.

"Let's get this party started," Creed announces, and something like relief washes over Boris' face. Maybe he wasn't so sure of his welcome after all.

He digs deep into his coat pocket—so deep I find myself tensing, ready for anything. But it's just a phone he pulls out, sleek and black, the screen catching the light as he hands it to Creed.

"You ring," Boris says, pushing the device into Creed's palm.

Creed's fingers close around the phone. He scrolls through the contacts, but there's only one entry, a number without a name. He looks up at us, a silent question in his eyes. Reaper nods, his expression set in stone. I give a slight tilt of my head. No turning back now.

The call button is pressed, and the speakerphone is engaged. We gather around, the tension coiling between us like a live wire.

"Creed," comes the voice of Lev Ivanov from the speaker. There's a coldness to it that makes the hairs on the back of my neck stand up.

"Lev." Creed's voice is steady, giving nothing away.

"We've taken over the Diablos," Lev states matter-of-factly as if discussing the weather. "Consider these weapons a measure of good faith."

"Good faith," Creed echoes, skepticism lacing his tone. His eyes scan the arsenal before us, then flick back to the phone.

"Yours to do with as you wish," Lev continues, and the line crackles with the weight of those words.

"Understood." Creed's reply is clipped, and he ends the call with a decisive thumb press.

"Looks like we're back in business," Reaper murmurs, but his eyes are wary, watchful.

"Let's load up," Creed says.

This is more than a gift—it's a game changer. And in our world, change is rarely bloodless.

"Damn," I mutter under my breath.

"Let's move out," Creed barks as he pockets the phone.

Reaper nods, his eyes scanning the horizon like he's expecting trouble to roll up on us at any second. "Wheels up," Reaper yells, facing the woods.

Creed approaches Justice and points at his bike. "Move her off the road. Make sure she's hidden."

"Will do," Justice replies, his voice low as he walks toward Creed's pride and joy. He'll stash the bike where God himself couldn't find it.

Creed hoists himself up into the truck, then jangles the keys in his hand. "Let's move."

My bike roars to life, and we move into formation, Reaper and I falling in behind the truck.

The convoy rolls out, engines thundering as we put miles behind us.

***

Our procession slows as Creed takes the truck through our compound gates. I downshift, easing off as Reaper and I roll to a stop outside the gate.

A black SUV is parked near the entrance, a suit leaning against it. It's not until we dismount that he looks up and shows us his face.

"Trouble," I mutter, eyeing Hector.

He's normally always suited up, looking like Wall Street in a world of leather and tattoos. But not today. Today, he's a mess, a shell of the man who once stood by Camilla Sanchez's side. His eyes are bloodshot, with visible veins crisscrossing the whites, giving him a weary appearance.

"Reaper," he rasps, nodding at my VP with something that looks like respect.

"Creed..." I call out. "You've got company."

Creed gets out of the truck, his face a mask of stone. He strides over with Winchester and Justice on either side of him. Hector waits, holding back words until Creed's within striking distance. You can cut the tension with a knife.

Before Creed can speak, Hector holds up a hand. His voice is rough as he speaks, "They killed her." He pinches his nose at the bridge and waggles a finger in Creed's direction. "I don't blame you." Hector looks at Creed. "She couldn't get over your rejection of her. Her pride was her downfall. What Camilla did, going against you, it shouldn't have happened." He shakes his head. "You cut the head off the snake..." Hector finally says, his voice hollow, "... but another will rise."

"Is that right?" Creed asks.

"It won't be me. You've thrown in with the Russians, and they only care about themselves."

Creed says nothing. He crosses his arms over his chest and stares at Hector.

"The organization is already rallying. War's coming."

Creed frowns. "The Diablos picked the fight. We worked for you for years, and you betrayed us. Tried to force us out." Creed points at his chest. "I nearly got killed, and for what? Because Camilla felt jilted?"

"You made her look weak. She felt she had to strike back at you." Hector's bloodshot gaze searches each of us. "But I'm not here to discuss the past."

"Why *are* you here?" I ask.

Hector focuses on Creed. "You can't trust the Russians, and you were right. You did work for us for years, and for years, we had each other's backs."

"Until you tried to kill me."

Hector waves a hand in the air. "It's in the past.

Your MC controls Jacksonville. We *will* rebuild, and when we do, you'll have a decision to make."

"And if we side with the Russians?" Creed asks.

Hector slightly shakes his head, walks to the driver's side of his SUV, opens the door, and climbs in. Through the open window, he says, "I know you, Creed. You'll do what's best for the MC and your Devil."

Hector starts the car, and we stand together as he drives away.

"What the fuck?" Reaper asks.

"Yeah, what the fuck?" I repeat.

"I think it's Hector's way of letting us know he wants to do business with us again."

My eyebrows shoot up to my hairline. "Creed, you've gotta be fucking kidding me?"

Creed shrugs. "He's a businessman, and he's right... we do own the streets of Jacksonville."

Reaper chuckles. "Yeah, and now we're armed to the teeth to protect it."

Creed grins. "We sure are, but we don't need this much firepower. Winchester, reach out to the Irish and maybe the Khans. I see lots of green in our future."

Chapter 20

Highway

The scent of beer, oil, and leather hits me hard as I enter the clubhouse. I'm on a mission. My eyes scan the room, cutting through the haze of cigarette smoke and raucous laughter, searching for one face among the sea of brothers and their old ladies.

"Highway!" someone shouts, but I barely nod.

Not stopping.

Can't stop.

She's here somewhere.

The back of the clubhouse is where the noise dulls to murmurs and chuckles. That's where I find her—Lyric, my woman. She throws her head back, and a cascade of hair tumbles around her face as she laughs at something Jet says. Jet, with her dark hair and eyes that have seen too much.

My heart beats a little faster at the sight of Lyric.

It's love, pure and fierce. Seeing Lyric happy and hearing that uninhibited laugh feels like a jolt to my heart. "Hey, babe," I say as I approach.

Her laughter winds down, and those bright eyes lock onto mine.

"Highway," she greets, her smile still in place, like she knew I'd come looking for her, and she's been waiting.

"Jet." I nod, acknowledging her without taking my eyes off Lyric. She tips her chin up by way of a greeting.

Lyric turns in her seat, and I catch a glimpse of that spark in her eyes that tells me she's exactly where she wants to be—with me, with us, and in this life we've chosen, dangerous edges and all.

"Missed you," Lyric says, simple and true, like everything about us.

"Back at you," I reply, because what else is there to say?

There's a space next to her on the log, so I sit beside her. My hands find her waist, fingers gripping with a touch of ownership. With a fluid motion that's as natural to her as breathing, she's on my lap, perched like she belongs there because... *she does.*

With ease, I pull her closer. I'm rough around the edges, always have been, but with her, it's different. She leans back against me, a perfect fit, and I can't help but think how right it feels—a puzzle piece snapping into place.

Reaper strides in, Lucy tucked at his side, her bubbly personality a stark contrast to his dark presence. They're another piece, another perfect damn fit.

"Highway," Reaper nods, dropping onto the log across us like he owns it. His voice, a low rumble, cuts through the din of rowdy bikers and clinking glasses.

"Reaper," I acknowledge.

This is family.

This is brotherhood.

Lucy grins, eyes flicking to where Lyric sits on me. "Looks cozy," she says, her voice lilting with laughter.

"Life goals," I say with a smirk, watching them settle in. There's nothing but truth in those words.

My mind drifts for a second, Creed with Devil, Reaper with Lucy, all of us finding anchors in the storm. Rough men with hearts that beat fiercely for their women. The thought punches a grin onto my face, fierce and proud.

Justice strolls in, eyes scanning the area like he's casing the joint. He's got that look—cool, calculated, every inch the enforcer he is. But when his gaze lands on Jet, something shifts. It's subtle, but I catch it, the hard lines softening just a fraction.

"Jet," he says, his voice smooth as whiskey, pulling up a chair next to her with a confidence that's all Justice.

"Hey," she replies, and damn if she doesn't blush, her smile shy but lighting up her face.

"Having fun?" Justice asks, leaning in, close enough to share secrets or steal kisses.

"Yeah."

"Good." He grins and then holds out a beer for her.

Jet takes it, twists off the top, and clinks the bottle against his. The grin he's wearing grows bigger, and I see how much he likes the broken woman.

"Upstairs?" Lyric whispers against my neck, her breath hot, sending shivers down my spine.

"Lead the way, babe," I say, standing up, my hands steadying her as she slides off my lap, right onto her feet. We're a team, moving through the crowd, her hand clasped in mine, an unspoken promise between us.

The stairs creak under our boots, every step a beat closer to the haven above. The door to our room swings open, and we slip inside, away from the chaos, into our own slice of peace, just Highway and Lyric, the way it's meant to be.

The moment the door clicks shut, it's like a switch flips. My hands are all over her, pulling her close with an all-consuming hunger. She matches my intensity, her fingers tearing at my cut, the heavy leather falling onto the bed.

"Highway," she breathes out, and it's a spark right to my core.

"Lyric," I growl back, our lips crashing together, a collision of need and desire.

Her taste is intoxicating, sweet, and fierce, and I'm downing it like the finest whiskey.

Clothes shed like unwanted skin. We're bare, the moonlight spilling through the window painting her in silver.

"God, you're beautiful," I mutter against the valley between her breasts, my voice rough like gravel.

"Yours," she whispers, and that one word sends me over the edge.

Climbing onto the bed, I sit with my back against the headboard. Lyric climbs on me and slowly impales herself on my cock. I thrust up inside her, a relentless rhythm, and she's meeting me with every drive of my hips. The world outside doesn't exist—it's just us, tangled sheets, and the sound of our union filling the room. Sweat beads on our skin, the air charged with electricity, every touch sparking fire.

"Highway!" she cries out, her nails digging into my back, marking me as much as I've marked her.

"Lyric!" I echo her cry, my release tearing through me, a tidal wave that leaves nothing untouched.

We collapse together, a twisted mess of limbs

and satisfaction. Our breathing slows, hearts still pounding out a wild beat, a testament to what we've just shared. I cradle her against me, her head on my chest, the rise and fall of her breathing syncing with mine.

"Do you remember you promised me we'd escape on your bike?"

A smile creases my face, the memory of that night flooding back. "Sure do. The open road and no looking back."

"Do you think we could cut it short and take off for a week?"

"Why would we do that?"

"Highway..." she starts, her voice a soft murmur against my skin. "I've got news."

"Shoot," I say, my hand stroking her hair, the silky strands slipping through my fingers.

"I've been offered an assignment..." she says, and there's a tremble in her words. "A photographic gig in Ukraine to document the war. They want me to leave in eight days."

The words hang in the air, heavy as lead. War zones are no playgrounds—they're hell on earth. But this is brave, unstoppable Lyric, and if anyone can capture the chaos and beauty of life in the midst of destruction, it's her.

My hands ball into fists, tension builds in my chest like a coiled spring. "Ukraine's a goddamn war zone, Lyric. It ain't safe."

She nods against me, her resolve a tangible thing. "It's important, Highway. To show the world." Lyric grabs my hand, her grip strong and unyielding. "This is about my goals and my life outside the club."

"Your life is here, with me," I say, the words barreling out before I can stop them. The thought of her in some distant battlefield, camera in hand instead of my fingers entwined with hers, it twists my gut.

"Highway." Her voice softens, and she traces the tattoo on my arm. "I love you. You're the man I want, the only one." She leans closer, her breath warm against my cheek. "But this... this is something I need to do. You understand chasing something that matters, don't you?"

Her words hit me like a punch to the gut, and I'm silent, grappling with the tightrope between my need to protect her and my respect for her passion. The room suddenly feels too small, the walls closing in as the weight of her confession settles over me.

"Lyric..." I start, but the words don't come.

How do you argue with a woman who has dreams bigger than any horizon I've ever chased?

"Hey," she says, a small smile playing on her lips, the kind that tells me she's not asking for permission, more like she's telling me what *will* be. "This is important to me. As important as the club is to you. Can you understand that?"

And dammit, I do.

Because if there's one thing I get, it's the call of the road, the pull of something that's in your blood. And Lyric has the heart of a rebel and the soul of an artist, painting stories with her lens in ways most folks can't even dream of.

"All right, baby," I say finally, pulling her back into my arms. "A week of you and me on the open road. Then you go and do what you gotta do."

Her kiss is all fire and promise, stoking a different kind of flame that speaks of wild love and the kind of devotion that doesn't chain you down but sets you free. Free to chase the thunder, ride the storm, and always, always come back home.

Yeah, life with Lyric isn't ever going to be normal. But then again, who the hell wants normal? Not me. Not when I've got a love that burns hot enough to rival any blaze she'll find in a war zone.

Life's going be one hell of a ride, and I'm strapped in, ready for wherever this road takes us.

Together or miles apart, we're in it full throttle, no brakes.

And I wouldn't have it any other way.

Chapter 21

Lyric

The room's still dark, only the soft glow of the moon filtering through the curtains. Highway's breath is slow and steady beside me. His arm, a heavy band over my waist, pins me to the bed, safe but caged. Hunger gnaws at my stomach, a different kind of need. I slide his arm off with a careful touch, afraid to wake the beast.

His black T-shirt is on the floor. I pick it up and tug it over my head—it hangs loose. Highway's scent clings to it, and I breathe it in. In bare feet, I creep down the stairs, silent on the cool wooden planks. The kitchen awaits, shadowy and still.

With a flip of the switch, harsh light floods the space. I rummage through the refrigerator—bread, cheese, leftover chicken—and my stomach growls with approval.

I glance out the window, drawn by the flicker of flames. There's Jet, her silhouette illuminated by firelight. She sits among the women we snatched from hell's jaws, their faces ghostly in the dance of the fire. They're laughing, the sound distant but real. A semblance of freedom they're only now tasting.

Justice is there, too, a hulking shadow detached from the rest. He's close to Jet, close enough to feel her warmth. A protector or something more? Even from this distance, I can see the tension between them.

My hands are busy making a sandwich as I watch them. Quietly, I chew on the edge of my sandwich, but the taste is bland, so I open the refrigerator, pull out the mayonnaise, and lather it on one side of the bread.

I lean against the cool granite kitchen counter, sandwich in hand, eyes fixed on the world outside. Jet stands up and stretches. She throws her head back, and the firelight catches her face, transforming her. Gone is the tremor in her posture, the shadow of fear in her eyes.

She's reborn from the ashes, fierce and defiant.

The woman looks like a phoenix, rising and reshaping herself before our very eyes.

Jet laughs, a sound rich that's unburdened, and

tosses her hair, dark strands glowing ember-red in the flickering light.

My gaze shifts, finding Justice. He's like a statue carved out of the night itself. But his eyes, they're alive, burning with a focus so intense it could set the world ablaze. And every ounce of that focus is riveted on Jet.

He doesn't blink or move. He watches her like she's the first and last thing he'll ever see, as if she hangs the moon just for him. A smile tugs at the corner of my mouth. Justice, the hard-ass with a heart of molten gold, melted by a woman who clawed her way back from hell.

I take another bite of my sandwich—the mayonnaise was a good addition. I push away from the counter, feeling like a peeping tom. Their story isn't mine to watch.

"Peacock and phoenix," I mutter, taking a bite. I wipe crumbs off my fingers, thinking about how we all look for someone to anchor us in the storm. Maybe Justice has found his anchor. Maybe they've both found something worth clinging to.

With my T-shirt hanging off me like a banner of the life I've chosen, I turn away from the window. It's time to slip back into the quiet of the bedroom and Highway's arms. He's my harbor and safe haven in the night.

Casting one last look at Justice and Jet, I smile to

myself because if anyone can handle a peacock, it's a woman reborn from flames.

The END

Also, in
The Royal Bastards MC Jacksonville FL Series
Creed Book 1
Reaper Book 2
Highway Book 3

More books
TO CHECK OUT

The Savage Angels MC Series

Savage Stalker Book 1
Savage Fire Book 2
Savage Town Book 3
Savage Lover Book 4
Savage Sacrifice Book 5
Savage Rebel (Novella) Book 6
Savage Lies Book 7
Savage Life Book 8
Savage Christmas (Novella) Book 9
Savage Release Book 10
Savage Heart Book 11
Savage Angels Book 12
Savage Angels MC Collection Books 1 – 3
Savage Angels MC Collection Books 4 – 6
Savage Angels MC Collection Books 7 – 9
Savage Angels MC Collection Books 1 - 9

Highway

The MacKenny Brothers Series
An MC/Band of Brothers Romance

Spark Book 1
Spark of Vengeance Book 2
Spark of Hope Book 3
Spark of Deception Book 4
Spark of Time Book 5
Spark of Redemption Book 6
Spark of Passion Book 7
Spark: MacKenny Brothers Series Books 1 - 3

The Tackling Series
Tackling Love Book 1
Tackling Life Book 2

Standalones
Wraith
Fealty: A Wraith Novel
Cardinal: The Affinity Chronicles Book 1
Snake's Revenge: Gritty Devils MC

Kathleen Kelly

,

Connect With
ME ONLINE

Check these links for more books from
Author Kathleen Kelly

READER GROUP
Want access to fun, prizes and sneak peeks?
Join my Facebook Reader Group.
https://bit.ly/32X17pv

NEWSLETTER
Want to see what's next?
Sign up for my Newsletter.
https://www.subscribepage.com/kathleenkellyauthor

BOOKBUB
Connect with me on Bookbub.
https://www.bookbub.com/authors/kathleen-kelly

Highway

GOODREADS

Add my books to your TBR list
on my Goodreads profile.
http://bit.ly/1xsOGxk

AMAZON

Buy my books from my Amazon profile.
https://amzn.to/2JCUT6q

WEBSITE

https://kathleenkellyauthor.com/

TIKTOK

https://www.tiktok.com/@kathleenkellyauthor

TWITTER

https://twitter.com/kkellyauthor

INSTAGRAM

https://instagram.com/kathleenkellyauthor

EMAIL

kathleenkellyauthor@gmail.com

FACEBOOK

https://bit.ly/36jlaQV

About THE AUTHOR

Kathleen Kelly was born in Penrith, NSW, Australia. When she was four, her family moved to Brisbane, QLD, Australia. Although born in NSW, she considers herself a QUEENSLANDER!

She married her childhood sweetheart, and they live in Toowoomba.

Kathleen enjoys writing contemporary romance novels with a little bit of steam. She draws her inspiration from family, friends, and the people around her. She can often be found in cafés writing and observing the locals.

If you have any questions about her novels or would like to ask Kathleen a question, she can be contacted via email:
kathleenkellyauthor@gmail.com
or she can be found on Facebook. She loves to be contacted by those that love her books.